His Irreplaceable Belle

His Irreplaceable Belle

A Touches of Austen Novella

LEENIE BROWN

LEENIE B BOOKS
HALIFAX

Cover design by Leenie B Books. Images sourced from Deposit Photos and Period Images.

His Irreplaceable Belle © 2020 Leenie Brown. All Rights Reserved, except where otherwise noted.

ISBN (print) 978-1-989410-57-8; (ebook) mobi: 978-1-989410-56-1

Contents

Dear Reader,

This novel is part of my *Touches of Austen* Collection of Austenesque stories. These stories feature original characters and plots that have been touched in some way by the influence of Jane Austen and her novels.

Since *His Irreplaceable Belle* is a story about separated lovers getting a second chance, you may have (correctly) guessed that this book and its main characters pay homage to Jane Austen's *Persuasion*. While there are intentional nods to Miss Austen's work in this story, there may also be some which are purely serendipitous or might make you think of a completely different Austen novel.

If you would like to share your observations about which elements you thought were Austen-inspired, you can do that in my *Touches of Austen Readers Group* on Facebook.

Happy Reading!

Chapter 1

Fredrick "Fritz" Norman had just picked up his pen and begun to record his observations about his most recent patient when the door to his surgery opened. He looked up, intending to give a nod of greeting to his visitor before returning to his writing. But the sight of the person who had stepped inside his office caused his pen to stutter on the page.

She was not supposed to be here. In fact, at present, if he had to choose one patient he did not wish to have enter his surgery, it would be her, for he was attempting to avoid her.

Quickly, he placed his pen in its holder before he could make a further mess of his notes. There would be no returning to recording his thoughts while Mrs. King was present. She was a lovely woman, but she was demanding and did not like to wait.

"Mrs. King, I had not thought to see you." He pushed up from his desk.

Mrs. King was not one of the patients who called on him at his surgery. She did not need to pay him in feed for his horse or eggs for his breakfast. She kept him on a retainer and expected him to call on her once a week to hear about whatever ache or pain was plaguing her at that moment. She was in good health and had no dire need of medical attention. All she really needed was for him to assure her that she was not ill.

"You have not called in two weeks."

That had been purposefully done, though he was not about to admit that to her.

She removed her reticule from where it hung on her wrist before skewering him with a critical look. "I could have died in that time, and you would not have seen me at all."

"You are not dying. You are amongst my healthiest patients." He motioned for her to take a seat in the chair that was in front of his desk. It was turned at an angle so that he might approach his patients from the front, but, if need be, with a turn of the head, a patient could also hold a conversation with him while he sat and wrote notes.

"I will not be in such good health if you continue to ignore me." She sat as indicated, and her lips pursed and her brows rose as a look of great displeasure settled over her features.

"I have not ignored you." Avoiding was not the same as ignoring. "I have sent Mr. Spencer in my place. I assure you that he is an excellent assistant and his reports are most thorough."

"I will not see him. I wish for a physician, not a surgeon. It matters not to me how fine Mr. Spencer is."

Fritz blew out a breath. He had had a suspicion that his assistant being sent away completely yesterday without even gaining entrance to Mrs. King's residence was a sign that he would need to find someone else entirely to take on her care.

"I have a couple of meetings arranged with other physicians. Mr. Spencer was just a temporary measure to see that you were well while I found you an appropriate replacement for my services."

Mrs. King's gaze roamed over Fritz's face. Then, she shook her head. "That will not do. I shall see you or no one at all. Do you wish to be the cause of my deteriorating health?"

"You are in excellent health, Mrs. King. I am certain you could sustain a period of time without weekly calls by a physician."

She adjusted the hem of the glove on her right hand. "But I do not wish to go without those calls, and I will have no one but you. I shall raise my payment by ten percent." She opened her reticule and drew out a banknote. "Do you wish for me to leave this with you or your man of business?"

"I have no man of business." Which she knew for they had discussed that very thing not more than a month ago, and Mrs. King's memory was as sharp as any he had seen.

"Then, I shall leave this with you, and you can call on me tomorrow."

"I cannot do that." For that would mean seeing her niece, and he truly could not bear that.

She studied him again for a long silent minute. "Why?"

"I just think it would be best if you were under the care of another." It would most certainly be best for his peace of mind.

Her expression told him that she did not think it

would be better. "Is this new physician I am to see better than you?"

"Perhaps." He was not so arrogant as to think there could not be a better physician than he, but he also was not so self-abasing that he would refrain from declaring his skills as finely honed.

"Can you guarantee that he is? For, from what I have been told by Mr. Blakesley, there is none better in Bath than you."

The praise of a friend was supposed to be something for which one should feel grateful. However, at the moment, grateful was not the feeling coursing through Fritz's veins. Dread, fear, the feeling of being backed into a corner and held at gunpoint – all of those were much closer to the way he was currently feeling.

"No, I cannot guarantee that. While I do believe my friend puts greater faith in my abilities than even I do, he is not wrong in saying that I am good at what I do."

Mrs. King smiled rather triumphantly. "Well, if that is the case, then, I should like a reasonable explanation as to why I should be placed in inferior care when I am paying for the best. If you cannot give me one acceptable reason to quit me, then you must remain as you have been – my physician." She placed the banknote she held on his desk. "With a ten percent increase in your fee."

He picked up the banknote and held it out to her. "I can neither give you a good reason, nor can I accept this."

She shook her head. "You can and you will accept it. I will have it no other way, and you surely must know that a disappointment at my age is a perilous thing. It would not do at all for me to take to my bed with malaise when I have a niece who needs to visit the Upper Rooms and the theatre." She stood.

"And how," she added with a charming smile – she must have been a very popular lady in her youth – "when I am bedridden, am I to take a walk in the Gardens to take in the air and enjoy the brightness of the day? It does so much good for one's health, or so I have been told by the best physician in Bath."

It was just like her to use his words against him. She was like Blakesley in that regard – both were prodigiously good to him until they wanted something, and then, they would sway him by repeating his own wisdom to him. He shook his head. There was no way he was going to be allowed to quit his place as her physician.

"I will have an apple cake," she said with a smile and a waggle of her eyebrows. "Cook is making it first thing tomorrow as I expect Mr. and Mrs. Blakesley to call."

Very carefully, she placed her reticule back on her arm. "I should think that if you were to call half an hour before regular calling hours begin, you would be able to take tea and eat cake with your friends. I find it is always a better time when there are several good friends gathered." She stopped at the door to his surgery which he opened for her. "And I do consider you a friend, Mr. Norman."

"I thank you for your consideration."

"No thanks is needed. One does not befriend another to receive thanks." She shook her head as if it was the daftest thing she had ever heard.

"Now, Annabelle," she said to the pretty lady who had risen from the chair in the hall outside his surgery, "we have a garden to visit. Do not dawdle. A brisk walk is best for one's constitution. It makes the heart hardy and hale and gives vibrance to the cheeks. Is that not what you tell me?"

Apparently, he was not the only one to have his

words of wisdom tossed back at him by Mrs. King when she wished to have her way.

"Yes, Aunt. Thank you for seeing my aunt without an appointment, Mr. Norman." She gave her aunt a pointed look.

"Mr. Norman is a friend. One calls on a friend as one feels led. I needed no appointment." Her smile slipped into a smirk. "Besides, his appointments were concluded for the day. I was not delaying him from another."

"How did you know that?" Fritz asked.

"I saw Mr. Spencer leaving upon my arrival."

Oh! She was cunning.

"From the sounds of your niece's advice, Mrs. King, you do not need my care. I think you would do well enough without me."

"And not have a handsome young man to simper over me?" She chuckled. "I think not. Come along, Annabelle."

"Thank you," Belle whispered once more before adding, "your attention means a lot to her."

"So it would seem," Fritz muttered.

"I am very glad to see that you have done so well." She gave a sweeping look around the hall and through the door to his surgery before scurrying away when her aunt called to her from the door to Fritz's townhouse.

He watched her exit, and then returned to his surgery to finish making the notes he had been writing when Mrs. King entered. However, he did not cross immediately to his desk. Instead, he chose to peek out the window and watch Mrs. King and her niece make their way down the road.

As he watched them, Belle looked back. Fearful of being caught watching, he stepped back but did not give up his observation of her. How could he? His heart was as drawn to her now as it had been six years ago. He sighed and allowed himself to feel the agony of a longing which would never be satisfied. Then, when he could see them no longer, he continued to his desk and dropped into his chair.

His pen was waiting for him, and he knew he needed to finish his notes. Yet, his mind was not ready to return to the improvement of Mr. Weller's leg pain when exercise and rest were taken in proper measure. There was no room to contemplate the role proper meals and limited sweets had played in Mr. Weller's improvement. There was not even space to chuckle over the consternation expressed by Mr. Weller over the grievous lack of sweets in his home.

Fritz's mind was filled to overflowing with thoughts of Mrs. King's beautiful niece and the puzzle of how he was going to be able to call on Mrs. King and not feel his heart constricting each time he had to sit and take tea with Belle.

He dropped his head into his hands. Surviving such a call while Belle remained unattached would be painful enough, but what would he do when she had callers? How would he be able to tolerate seeing other fellows fawn and flatter her? And he knew they would. How could they not? Belle was as pretty now as she had been when he last saw her six years ago. She was much sought-after then, and he was certain she would be just as sought-after now.

He expelled a slow breath in an attempt to alleviate some of the deep ache in his heart. The thought of another gentleman courting Belle was as disagreeable now as it had been every time it had crossed his mind over the past six years.

He needed a remedy, some sort of prescription.

He leaned back and looked up at the ceiling. What would cure a broken heart? There were tonics on the apothecary's shelf or in the liquor cabinet in his home which could dull the pain, but none of those would cure it.

He tapped his fingers on the arm of his chair.

Love.

That seemed the only thing which might do it. But where would one find such a tonic? Fritz had not met one lady of what he considered the proper age who captured his attention. And he had looked. Every season, with each new influx of temporary residents, he had looked.

He scrubbed his face. He knew that if a patient were ill and if the right tincture was not available and could not be created, he would look to other solutions even if they were new and had not been rigorously tested.

He blew out a breath. That was what he would have to do since the perfect remedy for his heart – someone who was as old as Belle, as pretty as Belle, and as practical as Belle – was not something that was available to him. He would have to look to a newer remedy.

He scrubbed his face again.

"A younger lady," he told himself. "You must consider a younger lady." Surely, there would be one who was not squeamish and given to fainting if he forgot himself and brought up a topic considered less than delicate.

Belle had never been one to look faint or horrified if he mentioned some particular experiment which he had witnessed while assisting Dr. Darby in town. She had always found even the most gruesome bits to be of great interest. For all her beauty – and she had a great deal of it, even now when her bloom should be fading – it had not been her beauty alone which had captivated Fritz.

What had called to him was her mind. It was inquisitive and quick. She would ponder the things he had told her about his studies and would often come back to him with some remedy which she had learned at the side of Mrs. Codling, a trusted servant in the Chapman house and the one on whom her mother would call first when one of her children became ill.

There would never be another so perfect as Belle. He knew it in his heart. However, he also knew that such perfection was not to be his, for he could not take her away from her mother.

He did not care if she never saw her father again. That gentleman was a fool of the highest order and did not understand Belle's intelligence. In fact, Fritz had heard him caution her on more than one occasion to keep her knowledge to herself so that she would not frighten away a good prospect by being labeled a bluestocking.

However, Belle and her mother had always been close, and it was only the fear of never being allowed to return to her home and see her mother that had kept Belle from running away to Scotland with him. He could have just as easily set up a practice in the north where no one would know of the rumor's Belle's brother Andrew had started which had labeled Fritz as inept and had kept him from finding a new position when his time with Dr. Darby had come to an end.

He blew out a breath in resignation. Perfect or no, a replacement for Belle must be sought, so that his heart might, after all these years, finally find some measure of peace.

Chapter 2

Annabelle Chapman attempted not to look back at the house she and her aunt had just departed. However, the temptation was too great, and surreptitiously, she cast a glance over her shoulder.

"Is he watching us?"

Belle startled at her aunt's question. She had thought she was being careful.

"I am not blind, my dear," her aunt continued when Belle did not reply immediately. "Nor am I unfamiliar with the longing of a young heart."

"My heart is not so very young," Belle replied, neatly dodging her aunt's original question or so she hoped. She would rather not speak about Mr. Norman. It was bad enough that she was going to have to see him and hear about him.

"It is not so very old either," Aunt Augusta said with a laugh. "Now, tell me if he was watching us."

It seemed that speaking about Mr. Norman was not something Belle was going to be able to avoid.

"He was, but he is not any longer." Was it because he had seen her glance just as her aunt had? Was that why he had stepped away from the window so quickly?

"Do you really think it is wise to keep him as your physician?"

"I will tell you again what I have already told you five times. Mr. Norman is the best, and as you know, I like the best. You are just going to have to prepare yourself to see him on occasion."

How did one do that? How did a lady harden her heart against the sorrow which seeing him would bring? As much as she longed for Fritz to once again proclaim his undying love for her, she did not expect him to do so, even if her heart, the foolish thing, hoped he might be persuaded in time. However, that seemed more like a young girl's dream – the sort of dream which only came true when the girl was a creation made of ink and fancy who lived happily between covers of leather on a library shelf.

"Did he agree to see you willingly?" She doubted it. He had not called in two weeks and before that, he had only called briefly and refused to stay for a cup of tea. Aunt Augusta had groused and grumbled for a full hour on each occasion.

"No, but I did not expect him to do so." She and Belle turned into the Sydney Gardens. "I cannot blame him for being skittish. A gentleman can only repair his life so many times – and I imagine, it gets harder as one gets older. However, he has nothing to fear from me for he will never receive anything but praise from my lips."

"But Father –"

"Is a pompous bore. That man has always cared more for his appearance than he has ever cared for anything else, and your brother, Andrew, as improper as it might be to speak ill of the dead, was just the same."

She stopped in front of a bench. "A brisk walk is much better if is it interrupted by a bit of repose," she said as she arranged herself on the bench. "We are not making a complete circuit. We have gone as far as I wish to go."

With a sigh, Belle sank down next to Aunt Augusta, placed her reticule on her lap, and passed her hand over the embroidered pattern on it, enjoying the variety of sensations the dots and curves created against her fingers and palm.

There was no point in arguing with Aunt Augusta about the need for more exercise, for her aunt could be very recalcitrant when it came to doing what she wanted. That was how Belle had known that Fritz would agree to see her aunt again. Aunt Augusta would leave him no option.

In that way, her aunt and father were alike. They were both stubborn old goats. Aunt Augusta was likely the more stubborn of the two, for she seemed to be the only one in all of Belle's acquaintance who did not care how much she angered Belle's father. Everyone else did as Sir Allen said, but not Aunt Augusta. At least, she did not if she had a different notion about what should be done, which was most of the time.

"I believe you had a letter from your mother," Aunt Augusta interrupted Belle's reflection.

"I did."

"Is she well?"

Belle nodded. "She says she is."

"And does she miss you?"

That was a good question. "She said she does."

"But..." Her aunt looked at her expectantly.

"But, it was added as an afterthought at the end of the letter after she had told me all about how well Henrietta was progressing with her music and dance lessons. You can read the letter if you wish." Belle took the folded missive from her reticule.

"I am afraid the sun is not bright enough for that."

"Of all the preposterous things, Aunt Augusta! You do not even require spectacles to stitch until the lamps must be lit."

Aunt Augusta laughed. "Very well, it is not that I cannot read it. It is just that I do not wish to bother with reading when there are people to watch. Do you see that couple over there?" She pointed to a gentleman and lady who were walking arm in arm along the path to their left. "She is his sister. She is much admired, and he seems excessively protective of her." She looked at Belle and raised an eyebrow. "He can be very particular and is not afraid to voice his opinions about things if you understand my meaning."

"He is a fine-looking gentleman."

"Oh, to be sure. Tall, handsome, and with a bank account to match him in size and attractiveness. However, he is not for you."

Her aunt was correct about that. No gentleman would ever be for her ever again. She had given her heart to Fritz many years ago now, and he still had it, whether he wished for it or not. She could not love another for she loved Fritz. She had tried but without success.

That was why she was here — to learn how a lady lives on her own. Aunt Augusta had been widowed just eight years after marrying and had never married again. Nor did she seem as if she wished to remarry.

"His sister is just as handsome if a bit reserved."

"And, being the sister of such a wealthy gentleman, she is then an heiress, is she not?"

Aunt Augusta nodded. "That is why her brother is so protective, I would assume. There are fortune hunters here just as there are in London. There just might not be as great a number for Bath is not so grand as town."

No, Bath was not so grand as town, but, in Belle's opinion, it was lovely. Just as in town, the streets of Bath were busy and there never seemed to be a shortage of people to see wherever one went, but it was not as dreadfully depressing as London seemed to be. However, that was likely just her opinion of the place, for Henrietta seemed beyond excited to be taking in the season in town next year. Perhaps if Belle had not had her heart broken when she was there, she might have found it just as thrilling as her youngest sister did.

"What else did your mother say. Surely, the whole letter was not about Henrietta."

"Oh, no, of course, it was not. There was a bit of hope expressed about Sidney's prospects. It seems he has written home about the same young lady twice now – a Miss Lucy Gibbs – and Father approves of her." Apparently, Miss Gibbs had the right pedigree, fortune, and beauty to satisfy Sir Allen's exacting expectations for his children.

"Has he met her?" Aunt Augusta's gaze turned to Belle and away from watching the couple she had pointed out to Belle just moments ago.

"Yes, Mother said that Father returned from town with a glowing report of Miss Gibbs and a fine bottle of wine, which was a gift from Miss Gibbs's father." Belle's father had been gone when she left home to come to Bath, and she had been glad of it. It meant that she had been seen off by just her mother and Henrietta, who were too kind to mention how she was wasting her looks on spinsterhood.

"Well, then, Miss Gibbs is as good as married to our Sidney. I assume he is still attempting to please your father."

"Very much so."

Sidney was now the heir to the baronetcy, unless, of course, her father cut him off and named Miles, who was their father's favourite, as heir in Sidney's stead.

"Why would he not?" she asked when her aunt shook her head in a disapproving fashion. "They have all heard of what happened to Mr. Norman, and Father has not been backward in making known his desire to be followed by a son who values the centuries-old traditions of our family."

"Well," Aunt Augusta said with a huff, "I hope Miss Gibbs is a sweet girl, for Sidney is not your father."

No, Belle's younger brother was more like their mother than their father, which was why he was so willing to please his father even when they did not agree.

"Judith is about to enter her second

confinement. As you might expect, she is hoping for a boy this time."

Judith, who was only a year younger than Belle, had been married since the summer after her first season.

"And both Mother and I hope she gets her wish," Belle added.

Judith had not become pregnant until three years after she married and had then been disappointed by the birth of a girl. It was not that she did not love her daughter. It was just that she worried about her husband not having a male heir because his property was entailed away from the female line.

"She worries far more than she should. Her husband will not see her or their daughters left without a home or an ample income. He seems a sensible sort."

And that was why Judith had not been home to visit her family more than once since she married. It was also why their father never mentioned Judith's husband without a shake of his head.

Fortune had shone on Judith for she had not only married a gentleman who had all the requirements their father desired but who also loved Judith madly and above all else. Nothing mattered more to him than his wife and now their daughter. To prove his devotion to Judith and their growing family, he had sold off a carriage to have some extra funds to invest once his daughter had been born. Sir Allen had not been pleased by the news, but Judith's mind had been eased.

Fritz would be that way. Belle knew it. He was a gentleman who, quite naturally, felt compelled to see to the needs of everyone, and whose compulsion to care for others only intensified when presented with the needs of someone counted among those whom he held dear. It was this caring and compassionate part of his nature which had first drawn Belle to him and had recommended him to her as a gentleman with a promising future. He had not had much in the way of wealth and worldly possessions when they had first met, but she had known, to the depths of her soul, that it was only a temporary state for him. She had always believed he would be a great success, and from what she had seen today and had heard since she arrived in Bath, her assessment had been correct. He was a success and would continue to be so.

Oh, to be a part of his life and cheer him on to further greatness as his wife! Her heart still cried for what had been lost. It ached with its desire to be the lady at his side. But how could she be? Why would a gentleman who had been so wronged ever wish to be tied to the very family who had threatened to deny him of his profession? Was not his reticence to continue his care of her aunt proof of that very thing?

"Was there any news of Miles?"

"Not much. However, he has not been dismissed from school, so things must be well with him."

From an early age, Miles, Belle's youngest brother, had been spoiled by their father. In their father's eyes, Miles could do no wrong, even when, in actual fact, he was doing wrong. He had a thirst for frivolity that seemed unquenchable.

Be that as it may, Annabelle could not help but smile at the thought of him. He was delightful. While he might be overindulged, his was not the sort to lord his good fortune over others. He was far too amiable for that. And since he had no reason to fear their father, he was always relaxed and playful. Many a tale of his escapades, told in his charming fashion, had brought a smile to Belle's face, even on the darkest of days.

"It is good to see you smile," her aunt said. "You do it far too little. Your smile has always been your most beautiful feature, and, my dear, dear niece, that is no small feat when there are so many other beautiful things about you with which it must compete."

Belle slipped her hand around her aunt's elbow and down to her hand, which she grasped. "Perhaps you can teach me how to smile as I used to?"

Her aunt squeezed Belle's hand. "I shall try my very best," she assured her before rising. "I find I grow weary of this aspect, so perhaps it is time to wander toward home?"

"That sounds lovely," Belle agreed.

"Of course," her aunt said as they began walking toward the entrance to the gardens, "I would not be opposed to stopping at a shop or two on our way."

"I think two would be the perfect number," Belle agreed. Hopefully, one of those shops would sell lace and ribbons, for she could use a bit more of both to finish the dress she had begun sometime before she had arrived at her aunt's house.

Her aunt chuckled. "This, my dear, is why we are so perfectly matched."

Chapter 3

The late afternoon sun felt wonderful and warming as Fritz turned his face towards it. The brightness that filtered through his eyelids was restorative. It had always drawn him forward from his often deep ponderings with a cheerfulness that was unparalleled by anything else, save for the smile of a particular lady.

However, he was not sitting in the garden to think about Belle. He was here to clear his mind and turn it towards the task at hand – finding a wife who was not Belle.

He drew a deep breath and released it. But neither the freshness of the spring air nor the intensity of the sun could chase away the dark shadow of sadness that passed across his heart at the thought.

"Mr. Norman."

Fritz straightened himself and opened his eyes. "Mrs. Blakesley." He stood.

"Please call me Grace. I think we will be good enough friends for such familiarity." Grace Blakesley took a seat on the bench next to where Fritz had been leaning backward and enjoying the sunshine. "My husband does not mind if you call me by my Christian name, do you, Walter?"

Walter Blakesley chuckled as he shook his head. Was there a happier man in all of Bath? Fritz was certain he had not seen one – not even Mr. Clayton and Mr. Shelton, who were each, without a doubt, happily and contentedly married and awaiting the arrival of a child, shone quite like Blakesley did. Joy effused every part of Blakesley's person.

"You may call my wife whatever she wishes for you to call her."

"I hate to disappoint your wife, but I may have to insist upon Mrs. Blakesley," Fritz said. "I assume you will not be discharging me as your physician, Blakesley, will you be?"

Blakesley guffawed. "And give up the best physician in Bath? I think not!"

A rather grumbly part of Fritz's mind wished

that people would stop referring to him as the best physician.

"Then, I assume you will also call on me if Mrs. Blakesley should ever be in need of care?"

"Of course." The answer was given without a moment's pause.

"In that case, Mrs. Blakesley, I will have to insist upon calling you Mrs. Blakesley. It would be too improper for us to be on friendlier terms."

Mrs. Blakesley scowled. "I do not see why it should be considered improper."

"There are many strictures which might seem ridiculous and yet we must abide by them. I would not wish to be thought of as unprofessional or lacking in decorum in any fashion."

Mrs. Blakesley's eyes grew wide. "Oh, yes, right. I completely understand." She paused to peek at her husband who had finally taken a seat next to her rather than standing and surveying their surroundings.

The man was incurably curious.

"Mrs. Blakesley is a lovely name," his friend's wife said happily. "I quite like it."

"I am glad to hear it," Blakesley said.

"As am I," Fritz inserted before the two with him forgot he was there.

Mrs. Blakesley turned back to him with a very serious look on her face. "I must apologize to you."

Fritz's brow furrowed. She needed to apologize to him? For what?

"Have you done something to me of which I do not know?"

She shook her head. "No, you know about it. In fact, you were agreeable to it, but I should not have asked you to take part if I had known."

He was thankful that the lady next to him was his friend's wife and not his. Such partial revelations were excellent at trying his patience.

Mrs. Blakesley leaned a fraction of an inch closer to him and lowered her voice. "My husband," she whispered, "has told me about what happened to bring you to Bath."

Fritz looked from her to Blakesley.

"I would never speak a word of it to anyone other than Grace," Blakesley assure him.

Fritz breathed a sigh of relief.

"Unless, of course, it was necessary to see you happy."

And the uneasiness Fritz had felt at Mrs. Blakesley's confession returned.

"We would never harm you," Mrs. Blakesley assured him, and without hesitation he trusted her words to be true.

It startled him how easily he believed her, but then she had such an open nature about her.

"And that is why I must apologize. I should not have asked you to play the part of my suitor – not even if the reason was an excellent one."

"I do not see a need to apologize for my agreeing to take part in your scheme."

She sighed. "But I told you that my mother would never approve of you and my sister would never attempt to steal you away because of your profession." She winced as she finished her sentence. "It was poorly done."

Ah, he understood now. "How could you have known I had been rejected for my profession?"

"You are too kind," Mrs. Blakesley cried. "I am certain my mother is not so unique as to be the only lady in all of England to think a physician is below her daughters – not that both of her daughters agree with her," she hastened to add in a flustered fashion. "I should have known it was a possibility that you had been treated shabbily before, and I should not have put you in a position to have to be reminded of that."

"I knew what I was doing when I agreed to help you." He smiled and nodded at his friend. "I could endure far worse for a friend."

"You must let me help you in return."

Uneasiness settled over him once again as he turned his full attention back to Mrs. Blakesley. "What do you mean? How do you plan to help me?"

"Why I shall help you find a wife, of course!" She said it as if it was the most natural and wonderful thing in the world.

"I am sure I do not need help."

Blakesley laughed.

"I am quite certain of it," Fritz retorted.

"Are you married and have not told me?" Mrs. Blakesley batted her lashes at him.

"No, I am not married."

"Are you courting anyone?" Again, she batted her lashes and looked at him as if he were an utter simpleton.

"No, I am not."

"Is there anyone you wish to court?" She held

up a finger. "Allow me to rephrase that. Is there anyone other than the lady you love whom you wish to court?"

"I am not in love."

"That was not the question," Blakesley inserted.

What Fritz would not give to be able to rise, inform his companions that he had somewhere to be, and leave this discussion. It could not end well. It just could not.

"No, I have not found anyone to court."

"Then, I fear you are wrong in this, Mr. Norman. You do, indeed, need help."

"No, I am certain I do not," Fritz repeated.

Mrs. Blakesley's expression grew grieved. "Are you truly going to deny me both the opportunity to repay your kindness and allow me to pay for my sin?"

"You have not sinned, and I did not help you to receive any payment."

"I told you he would say that," Blakesley muttered. "He is a physician but not because he wishes for the accolades of those he helps."

"Well, then, I shall not do it as a payment for services rendered. I shall give it to you as a gift." Mrs. Blakesley pulled herself straight and gave him a look that dared him to disagree with her. "You cannot refuse a gift. It would be most impolite."

"And, you would not wish to be thought of as unprofessional or lacking in decorum in any fashion," her husband added.

Of all the rotten things to do! Of course, Blakesley would throw Fritz's own words back at him. That was twice today that things he had said had been used against him. He shook his head. "I wish you would stop doing that," he grumbled.

"Doing what?" Mrs. Blakesley asked with a none-too-convincing innocent smile.

"Twisting my words to force me to do what you wish."

"I am certain I have not done something so vulgar as that!"

"Not you," he hastened to assure her. "Your husband is adept at it."

"He is rather clever, is he not?"

"I would rather not agree with that."

"Agree or disagree, it matters not to me what you think," Blakesley said with a taunting grin. "My wife thinks I am clever and that is all that matters."

There was no use arguing against his own logic, for if he did, he would end up calling Mrs.

Blakesley Grace since he would have to admit his argument about being more formal was wrong – which it was not! He must consider the particulars of the gift he was going to be obliged to accept. "If I agree to accept your gift, what will that entail?"

"Well," Mrs. Blakesley angled herself closer to her husband so that she might look at Fritz more directly, "there will have to be an interview." Her lips pursed. "Would you care to dine with us tonight or tomorrow? We could speak before we eat or during or, even, after."

"What sort of interview?"

"I have not known you too very long, so I must, you see, ask you about what you would like in a wife. Tonight would be best."

"Or we could just speak about it now," Blakesley inserted. "And you could still dine with us. I am not attempting to put you off or anything like that."

"I would not expect such treatment from you," Fritz assured his friend. Blakesley was as loyal and caring a friend as any gentleman could ask for.

"Do you think we could discuss it now?" Mrs. Blakesley asked eagerly. "I had thought to suggest it, but then, I thought it might be too forward to expect you to answer my questions without any warning that I had questions."

"Your concern does you credit, Mrs. Blakesley." What did it matter if he answered questions now or later? "What do you wish to know?"

"Will you join us for dinner tonight?" she asked.

"Tomorrow would be better. My cook would not be pleased to know that the fish she is preparing will not be eaten."

"You have a cook?"

"Yes. Does not every gentleman?"

Mrs. Blakesley smiled and lifted one shoulder. "I have never been intimately acquainted with a physician. We only had a surgeon and an apothecary in our village, though we did have a physician when we were in town. However, I have never considered how he lived. Truth be told, I only ever worried about whether he would make me drink some horrid tea or stay in bed when there were much better things to do."

Fritz could not help but chuckle at her comments. "We are known for imposing unpleasant cures on our patients."

"He has a cook, and a few other servants," Walter inserted. "He is not without an ample income. He is, after all, the best physician in Bath and rather astute when it comes to finances."

"Where do you live?" Mrs. Blakesley asked.

"Oh, not far from here," Fritz pointed in the direction of his house. "Just down there a bit. Close enough to walk through the gardens daily."

Her eyebrows had lifted. "And do you have a townhouse then?"

He nodded. "As would be expected, part of it is dedicated to my surgery, and I have two tenants for the season."

She blinked. "You do?"

Again, he nodded.

"Two tenants? So then, your home is not diminutive?"

"Not overly so. It is perhaps a shade smaller than Blakesley's."

"Huh." Her eyebrows were still lifted as she took in all of this startling information. "It is a good thing my mother did not know that, or she might not have been so opposed to you, for a townhouse is a good start. Huh," she said one more time as if she was still finding it hard to believe he had a townhouse and was not poor. "I suppose I should have asked more about you when we were dancing rather than always asking about my husband. But he is very handsome."

Fritz laughed. "Yes, I would have to agree that he is not a poor looking fellow."

"Oh, most certainly," she agreed. "Your living is comfortable?"

"Yes, very."

"Is it enough for a family?"

"Yes. I would not consider marrying if I could not provide for a family."

"That is very sensible," she assured him. "Well, then, shall we walk, and you can describe the sort of lady who would be your ideal companion?"

Describing his perfect wife would be both difficult and dead easy, for all he needed to do was describe Belle – without allowing his heart to grow so heavy that his true desire and the pain of denying it would be visible to all. He rose, and the Blakesleys joined him.

"Please walk with Grace," Blakesley offered. "It will make it easier for you to tell her what she wishes to know."

Fritz obliged and offered Mrs. Blakesley his arm. "My future wife must be sensible and not flighty. I like to discuss my research at times. Therefore, she must not be squeamish or given to fits of the vapors," he began.

"Oh, I would have never thought of that," Mrs. Blakesley cried, "which is why this interview was necessary. I imagine, then, that you have a great many things to study, do you not?"

For all her exuberance, Mrs. Blakesley was not without a keen, deductive mind.

"Yes, there is always something new about which to learn regarding the human body or new methods of treating illness, and then there are my own writings about things I have observed which must be contemplated and compared to the things I have read."

"Oh, my! You will want a wife to be quite intelligent then, will you not?"

"Ideally, yes."

"Must she know anything about medicine? I know some ladies are familiar with remedies. I myself have learned a few, though I admit to not having paid close enough attention to know many."

"It would be a great boon if my wife knew some common remedies – especially for the children. I cannot always be home." He looked off into the distance and attempted to not see Belle in his mind as he spoke.

"That is so sensible," she said softly and then fell silent.

They walked a few steps in silence.

"Do you wish to know what I hope she looks like?" he asked, glancing at her.

She shook her head.

That was surprising!

"May I ask why?"

Her face pinched and sadness filled her eyes. "You do not need to tell me, for I know with what she must compare."

He swallowed and turned his eyes away from her so that she would not see the sorrow he felt.

"That is the problem, is it not?" Blakesley said as he walked behind them.

Fritz nodded. That was, indeed, the seemingly unsolvable problem.

Chapter 4

Belle trailed a finger along the handrail which followed the curve of the staircase. Her aunt's home was beautiful. It was fresh and modern with a classical elegance that was welcoming. Ostentatious was a descriptor Aunt Augusta eschewed, for she said it reminded her far too much of her wig-wearing grandmother, as well as her self-absorbed younger brother. Therefore, she had made certain when she took this house to have it all redone to avoid anything which might smack too much of pretense.

Belle doubted there was likely much which had been pretentious about such a lovely and relatively new home like this one, but she did not truly care what the motivation was for how her aunt's home was decorated. She was just happy to be here, with her aunt and surrounded by fittings and fixtures that suited her tastes quite well.

"Mr. Blakesley, Mrs. Blakesley. It is good to see you," she greeted when she reached the bottom of the staircase and had entered the entrance hall. "My aunt will join us as soon as she has finished her appointment with Mr. Norman. We are to take tea in the garden sitting room today."

"Your aunt's home is divine," Mrs. Blakesley said as she followed behind Belle. "I know I said that the last time I was here, but I am so taken with it, I cannot help but repeat myself."

"I was just thinking the same thing mere moments ago," Belle said. There was much she liked about her new friend, but Mrs. Blakesley's tendency to thwart traditions at times and her expressive nature were likely two of the things Belle found most appealing.

"I am certain I would sit in each room for an hour and just take in every detail if I were to be the fortunate one who lived here." As she took a seat, her eyes followed the decorative molding along the top of the wall.

Mr. Blakesley chuckled. "She is not exaggerating. I still find her in one room or another of our home, admiring some bit of décor or architectural detail."

Belle could believe that. Mrs. Blakesley seemed the sort of lady who threw herself into all the things she loved. Belle could not imagine her new friend doing anything by half. She was delightfully passionate about those things she loved.

"They will become familiar and commonplace soon enough," Mrs. Blakesley said to her husband. "However, I do not wish to forget them when we move to Erondale. Therefore, I study them so I might commit them to my memory." She wrapped her hand around her husband's where it lay on his knee.

"Do you draw?" Belle asked, turning her eyes away from the pair in front of her, who were so obviously in love, and toward her hands for a moment to allow the prick of longing for such a future to fade.

"Oh!" Mrs. Blakesley cried. "I had not thought of drawing them."

"But, you do draw?"

"A little. Yes."

"I find it to be a delightful pastime," Belle agreed. "I particularly like studying plants."

"Then, you will have to visit us at Erondale this summer. The garden there is lovely, and I have not even seen it in full bloom yet."

"This house has a fine garden of its own," Mr. Blakesley said. "It is not extensive, of course, but it is well proportioned and designed." He rose and offered his hand to his wife. "I have seen you peeking at the window. Come see it for yourself."

"Oh, yes, you must see it," Belle agreed. "It is not as lovely as it will be, but it is still quite nice." She rose and joined them at the window which looked out to the garden below. "There is to be a new flower bed dug just at the edge of the area which is laid to lawn. I believe it is to be done next week and some rose bushes are to be placed in it. Aunt Augusta loves roses." They were flowers which were a bit like her aunt — beautiful but prickly.

"I do, indeed, love roses," Mrs. King agreed from the doorway, "Perhaps we can take a short amble through the garden after we have had tea."

"I would like that very much, Mrs. King," Mrs. Blakesley said as she turned away from the window.

Belle stayed as she was for a moment, looking

out at the green lawn and young plants. She needed a moment to compose herself before she faced him. She had been considering all morning how she would behave. She had finally settled on being friendly and as open as one could be when faced with the gentleman one loved but would never have. She must be herself. She could not become suddenly shy and retiring. Would she wish to be so all her life? She was certain she did not. Therefore, she must begin as she intended to be while living in Bath.

Having reminded herself of such thoughts, she turned to the room where the tea was being laid out on a small round table at which sat Mr. and Mrs. Blakesley, Mr. Norman, and her aunt.

"I am happy you could stay for tea, Mr. Norman," she said as she took her seat.

The man looked uncomfortably around the group.

"I suppose my aunt gave you little choice in the matter."

Ah, there was that small smile she remembered so fondly. The corners of his mouth would just tip up the tiniest bit. Normally, his eyes would also sparkle with amusement. However, just the small smile was enough for now. It was enough to give her hope of being able to pass a few minutes as friends or old acquaintances. Then the awkwardness between them might dissolve, and perhaps, with time, he would even come to forgive her for her family's wretched behaviour.

"She was rather insistent."

"She often is," Belle agreed.

"It is true. I am." Aunt Augusta lifted the lid off the teapot to inspect the contents. She always did, for she did not want to pour out tea which was sickly looking.

"Is it not ready yet?" Belle asked when her aunt took her seat rather than beginning to pour.

"It needs a minute longer to be how I prefer it. We will begin with cake." She picked up her fork, indicating that it was acceptable for everyone to eat. "Have you had any news from home?" She directed the question at Mrs. Blakesley.

"Just two days ago, I had a short letter from my mother, detailing all that is happening in the neighbourhood and which neighbors had called and such. Nothing of great importance." Her smile faltered. "Not yet," she added softly and to herself.

Belle wondered at her sadness. It always seemed to appear when speaking of her home.

"Did she mention plans for their trip to the seaside?" Aunt Augusta asked.

"I believe they will be installed in their cottage by tomorrow. She said that she has had a dress made for the occasion of their trip. "

"That is an excellent reason to have a dress made." Aunt Augusta was pouring tea and, with a small movement of one finger, indicated to Mr. Norman to whom he was to pass each cup.

Belle chuckled silently as she put a bite of cake in her mouth. According to her aunt, the sun rising in the morning was an excellent reason to have a dress made. That was one thing that Aunt Augusta shared with Belle's father – a prodigious love of clothing and fripperies.

"I have been attempting to persuade Annabelle to allow me to commission a dress for her, but she has yet to agree to it."

"I have a dress that is nearly finished, and Father made certain I had enough dresses before I left home."

Her aunt huffed. "Not a one of them is cheerful."

"They are practical and fitting for my station."

Just as she expected, the comment earned her a very pointed and disapproving look from her aunt.

"I am fond of blue, and grey is a calming colour," Belle added as she hid a small smirk behind her tea. Perhaps she should not goad her aunt as she was, but to do otherwise would not be being true to herself. Besides, her aunt enjoyed a bit of taunting, which was evident from the twitch of Aunt Augusta's lips.

"I can abide blue but grey?" Her aunt shook her head. "No one has died. It is not necessary."

"From what I remember, Miss Chapman looks lovely in both blue and grey."

The cup Belle held froze on her lips and neither poured any tea into her mouth nor sought to be returned to its saucer.

"Well…" Aunt Augusta's eyes were momentarily wide with surprise before she found her composure and continued, "Belle does look lovely in many colours."

"She does," Mr. Norman, who was carefully studying a crumb of cake on his plate and pushing it around with his fork while his ears burned a brilliant red, agreed softly.

Belle lowered her cup slowly, attempting to keep

the tremble she felt out of her hand, yet, despite her efforts, the cup rattled the tiniest bit when she placed it on the saucer.

"I would look dreadful in grey," Mrs. Blakesley said. "I am certain of it."

Her gaze held Belle's, and Belle recognized the gentle caring that lay behind the comments. Her friend was attempting to make what had been said into a natural turn in the conversation.

"It would depend upon the shade, I should think," Mr. Blakesley inserted. "I dare say there are shades of grey which would not look good on Miss Chapman either." He shrugged when all eyes turned his direction. "I have had material presented to me for a jacket and only one sample was truly flattering though they were all of the same colour by name."

"What colour was that?" his wife asked, her curiosity obviously aroused.

"Blue. It simply must be the correct shade and hue, or it is not becoming. I would venture a guess that the same is true with grey. A warmer grey with a green tinge or a golden undertone would likely suit you better than one that is too close to blue."

"I had not thought you a student of fashion, Mr. Blakesley."

"I know a thing of beauty when I see her," the gentleman replied to Belle's aunt without turning his eyes away from his wife.

Belle glanced at Mr. Norman who had moved from studying his plate to running a finger along the rim of his teacup.

He looked up at her just then and before his eyes could dart away, she forced herself to smile at him as a friend might smile at another friend who had paid her a compliment. Unfortunately, the action did not have the calming effect she had expected. Instead, he seemed more flustered than before.

He pulled his watch from his pocket. "I am expected somewhere soon," he said.

Belle's heart leapt to her throat. Had she offended him? Or had he remembered, after he had complimented her, who she was and what her family had done?

"Oh, you cannot leave yet," Aunt Agatha protested. "We were going to walk in the garden."

"I am afraid I cannot join you. I really must be on my way." He tucked his watch back in his pocket and, rising, gave a small bow first to the Blakesleys. "I will see you tonight."

"You had better see us tonight, or my cook will be displeased with the amount of food not eaten," Mr. Blakesley said.

"And I would miss your company," his wife said.

"I will be there," he assured her. Then, he bowed to Belle and then her aunt. "Miss Chapman, Mrs. King, I thank you for your hospitality."

His eyes shifted from Aunt Augusta to Belle, but all she could read in them in the brief moment during which they were on her was sadness. She supposed that was better than anger or disgust.

"I am sorry you must go, Mr. Norman," Aunt Augusta said. "However, I am pleased you joined us for so long as you were able." Her eyebrows rose. "I shall expect it again, just as has always been."

He paused before moving away from the table. "Are you certain you would not be willing to see –"

"I shall not hear of seeing anyone who is not you."

He nodded and darted one more quick glance in Belle's direction. "Then, I will see you again next week unless you find you are in need of my services before that time, though I doubt you will be."

And with that, he made his exit from the room.

Belle cradled her cup in her hands as she sipped its contents. Perhaps attempting to be as she always had been, had been the wrong choice. Maybe she should have remained quiet and reserved. Oh, what a disagreeable state of existence it was into which she had fallen!

She swallowed the last of her tea and returned her cup to the table just as Aunt Augusta began an inquisition into which flowers Mrs. Blakesley preferred.

While Mrs. Blakesley, without an ounce of success, attempted to come to the point of picking a favorite flower, Belle pushed away the troublesome thoughts of Mr. Norman and whether he and she could ever be in the same room without the air feeling frightfully heavy.

Belle smiled at Mrs. Blakesley's look of confusion over whether she should choose a happy flower or a beautiful one. She had new friends, lovely new friends, who would surely make enduring the moments of awkward unpleasantness of being disliked by Mr. Norman much more bearable.

Chapter 5

Of all the stupid things to do!

As he trudged down the busy street, Fritz swung his umbrella and imagined it dashing away his ineptitude in remaining unaffected in the presence of Belle.

Above him, the sky was a mix of blue and grey with the blue portion being larger than the grey at present. If only his life could become more clear than cloudy as quickly and easily as the heavens seemed to shift from threatening to favorable.

Why had he told Belle that he remembered how pretty she was in everything she wore?

He stepped to the side to let a sedan chair pass.

What an utter dolt he was! He shook his head. She had been startled by his admission – that was obvious! It had taken her several minutes to be able to look at him and smile sympathetically at his idiocy.

That smile.

His eyes closed as his heart squeezed small and retreated, attempting to hide from the longing he had felt at seeing *that smile* and the compassion in her eyes which was so much a part of her. How was he ever to find someone to take her place?

"Ah, Mr. Norman. Have you come to inspect the lot of us to see if we are following your directives?"

Fritz turned to the older gentleman who had joined him. "I am not certain I understand your meaning, Mr. Wesley."

Mr. Wesley, who leaned heavily on his cane, tipped his head to the right. "The Pump Room."

Fritz took in his surroundings. Chairs delivered people behind him while large columns on the face of the elegant building before him seemed eager to have him pass between them and enter with the others. He was indeed at the Pump Room, but how had he gotten here? This was not the direction in which he had intended to walk. He had intended to go home and spend a few hours in his surgery reading through his notes and writing a letter about his findings. Submersing himself in his work seemed a fine way to rid his mind of Belle, or, at least, it would occupy him so much that thoughts of her would be pushed aside for the time being.

"I have just arrived to take a meander around the place. That is, I shall meander after I have a sip of that foul-smelling water you claim will do me good and not hasten my demise."

Fritz's lips tipped up in amusement at his companion's testy tone. Mr. Wesley was always complaining about the instructions he was given. However, though the man would grumble loudly, he never strayed from what he was told to do. Would that all his patients were so compliant.

"Would I purposefully wish for your demise to the point of attempting to design its soon arrival?"

"That contraption you insisted I use twice a day seems precisely conceived to do just that."

"Does this grumble mean you are using your chamber horse as instructed?"

The man next to him grunted. "My wife will not let me do otherwise."

"You have married a good woman then." They stood just inside the door to the pump room. "Did she trust you to walk the room without her?" Fritz teased.

"No, she wanted me to take my exercise while watching her empty my purse on dresses and fripperies. I thought it better for my health to not be witness to the creation of bills such as I know she is capable of procuring." He shook his head. "She is a pretty thing, though. Always has been." A small smile – a very foreign thing for Mr. Wesley – graced Fritz's companion's lips for a half minute before he shifted his gaze to Fritz.

"How about you?" Mr. Wesley asked. "It is not good that man should be alone. Is that not how the scripture goes? I hear the pretty lady you were courting has married Blakesley. A fine fellow that Blakesley. I'd be hard-pressed to be too disappointed to lose a lady to the likes of him."

"I was not courting her," Fritz replied. "We were friends, and nothing more. I am actually quite pleased that she chose my friend over me. They are well-suited to one another."

"But that does leave you wanting," Mr. Wesley persisted. "However, I might be able to help you with that."

"I beg your pardon?" Had the grumbly old gent, hobbling along next to him as they made their way down the length of the Pump Room, just offered his services as a matchmaker?

"I have a granddaughter or two, and I have several friends with daughters and nieces and granddaughters and the like."

He had. Mr. Wesley had offered to find him a wife.

"My Charlotte is a fine young lady," the elderly gentleman continued, "She has had the best schooling, and her father and mother are not at all above themselves."

"Meaning they would condescend to allow their daughter to marry the likes of me?" That is what it often came down to, did it not?

"You know how some are." Mr. Wesley continued. "They think themselves equal to the prince and far too above anyone who is not titled or the heir to a great estate which was earned in the proper fashion –" his elderly companion leaned closer to Fritz and hissed his next words with disdain, "through birth."

Oh, Fritz knew all he ever wished to know about such people.

"We never taught our boy to be like that. His great grandfather was a mere farmer with a shrewd eye for advancement." He chuckled and winked at Fritz. This was perhaps the merriest Fritz had ever seen Mr. Wesley.

"He married a wealthy merchant's daughter," Mr. Wesley continued, "and invested in lands and livestock. You would be just the sort of fellow my grandfather would have liked. You are industrious and excel at what you do. I see a great future for you, and I believe it to the point of seeing you comfortably settled in a house of no small proportions, and such a home will need a mistress."

"I am content in my current dwelling." Not that he did not plan at some point to acquire something larger. His current townhouse would accommodate a small family quite well, but if he were to purchase a larger home while keeping and letting out his current home, he would have additional funds to add to the fortune he wished to amass for his children.

"Pah," Mr. Wesley waved Fritz's comment away. "Contentment is not without its merits, of course, but to be content with merely contentment seems a waste of your good sense and future fortune. My Charlotte is coming to visit me and Mrs. Wesley.

She will be here for six weeks. Volunteered to come help my wife and me. She is a kind-hearted young lady and quite eager to get away from some fop with little sense for more than how he looks in a jacket." His bushy brows rose. "She is quite sensible for being just nineteen as of last month."

"I am certain she is lovely, but..."

"I will introduce you. That is all. Nothing more. Just an introduction. I am not the sort to force a match. I would not wish to see my Charlotte in an unhappy situation."

"I think I can allow you to introduce her to me." Fritz was certain he had no choice but to allow an introduction. "However, I was hoping to find a wife who was a bit older."

Of course, as things stood, he should not be too fastidious about how young or old the ladies he met were. He just needed someone to fill the hole that had been left in his heart all those years ago.

"Charlotte is nineteen according to the church record, but she is, at least, three years older in temperament."

Mr. Wesley might not be interested in forcing a match between his beloved granddaughter and anyone, but, to Fritz, it appeared the gentleman was not above presenting her as a gem of an option.

"An introduction. That is all. I will agree to no more than that."

"That is all I ask," Mr. Wesley agreed. "However, I think you will be pleased to have made her acquaintance."

"Then, I shall look forward to meeting her." He was about to bow his leave when another of his patients inserted herself into the conversation.

"Who are you meeting?" Miss Philips asked.

"My granddaughter, Charlotte. He is in want of a wife, you know." Mr. Wesley answered on Fritz's behalf.

"I am not in want –"

"Oh, to be sure he is!" Miss Philips agreed without allowing Fritz to make his full protest.

He was in want of a wife. He knew that. There was no one by his side or waiting for him at home. However, it was not as if he were desperately in need. His head tipped. Then, again, if he thought about it, he might be a trifle desperate. The sooner he could find a wife; the sooner he could rid himself of the *what might have beens* that plagued him.

"Do you also have a suggestion for me?" he asked, causing both of his companions to look at him in surprise. "Mr. Wesley has offered up his granddaughter as a candidate, and since you, Miss Philips, seemed to agree that I need a wife as soon as can be, I thought you might have someone in mind."

The small lady, who always wore her hair in a tight bun covered by a simple cap with few embellishments, smiled slyly. "If I were thirty years younger, I would suggest myself. You are a handsome young fellow."

"Thank you."

"However, I am sadly too old which means I shall have to suggest my sister's daughter, Margaret. We are much alike, she and I, which has her mother concerned that she will not take – what with this being her third season and all."

A younger version of Miss Philips? That would not be too dreadful, he supposed. Miss Philips was a great conversationalist and not given to drama, for she was a practical woman. Excessively practical. Nearly to the point of being intolerably so.

"I would be happy for the introduction." He

really could not afford to be too particular. And a meeting was not an offer of marriage, he assured himself.

"She is just sitting there on that bench." Miss Philips indicated the general direction in which Fritz should look.

"In the green pelisse?"

"Yes, the very one."

She was tolerably pretty, but her beauty was not soul-stirring such as Belle's was – at least, it was not to Fritz. Margaret did resemble her aunt. She had fine features and a delicate frame. In fact, she looked as if a strong gust of wind might knock her down. However, if she was as much like her aunt as her aunt claimed she was, then the wind would have a great deal of convincing to do before it would be allowed to topple her. Miss Philips always needed proof and reassurance no matter what Fritz suggested would be the best way to progress forward in treating an ailment.

"I see no better time than the present to make the introduction." Fritz's comment earned him a pleased smile from Miss Philips.

"Do not forget that you are to meet my Charlotte," Mr. Wesley said. "Do not make a decision for three days. We will have tea after you call at my home, and you can meet my Charlotte as she will arrive the day after next."

"Well," said Miss Philips with a lift of her chin, "if he likes my Margaret, you cannot keep him from acting on such a thing."

"Like your Margaret above my Charlotte? I do not see that happening!"

"I would like to meet several young ladies before I make my choice," Fritz inserted. "A decision should have adequate research behind it."

Two pairs of eyes looked at him in shock.

"Choosing a wife is not the same as selecting a treatment plan, Mr. Norman," Miss Philips scolded. "No amount of research can tell you where a heart will find its home."

"I should say not," Mr. Wesley agreed.

"I still think it is best to meet a number of young ladies so that I can determine if my heart is playing me true or false. Emotions are fickle things."

Mr. Wesley shook his head. "It is no wonder you are still unmarried with logic such as that."

No, it was not logic that had kept him from marrying. It had been his heart.

"The heart knows what the heart knows

regardless of the head," Miss Philips assured him. "I once had the opportunity to marry, but I listened to my head instead of my heart, and well, as you can see, that did not work out so well for me."

"I am sorry to hear that."

"I was young and foolish. Do not be as I was," she cautioned as she placed her hand on his proffered arm and walked with him the few feet that separated them from her niece. "Follow your heart, even if it does not lead you to my Margaret, though I do hope it does. I should so love to call you my nephew."

"And I should like to have you for a grandson," Mr. Wesley, who was following behind them, said.

Two families who wished to have Fritz join their ranks. That was a new thing! It was a far more pleasant feeling to be sought-after than to be actively despised.

"Sister, I have brought him just as I said I would."

"You came to collect me?"

"Oh, yes. I was telling Margaret about you, and then I saw you, and well, it just seemed too fortuitously fortunate a coincidence to be anything other than destined that you should meet."

"I see," he said, though he truly did not see.

"Mr. Norman, this is my younger sister, Mrs. James, and her daughter, Miss Margaret James."

The young woman before him had a quick smile and lively amber eyes. He should not mind getting to know Miss James a bit better, even if it was just as friends. There was something about her which was intriguing.

"Sister, Margaret, this is my physician, Mr. Norman. He is a very *eligible* gentleman." She emphasized the word eligible, causing her niece to blush.

"It is a pleasure to meet you," Norman said with a bow, and not a word of it was a mere pleasantry which one must say to be thought polite, for it felt very much like a great pleasure to be meeting the niece of a lady who thought him a worthy choice for her sister's daughter.

Chapter 6

"Mr. Norman is such a dear friend," Mrs. Blakesley said as she and Belle strolled along the short path in Aunt Augusta's garden.

Belle smiled tightly and nodded in agreement with her friend's statement while wishing with all her heart that she and Fritz were friends as they had been years ago or even as he was with the Blakesleys now. However, based on how he had fled from her presence not more than a quarter of an hour ago, their relationship had been reduced from close friends and lovers to acquaintances who could never again be friends.

"I was very fortunate to find him upon my arrival in Bath. He helped me secure my husband you know."

Again, Belle nodded. She had heard the story of how Fritz had been instrumental in Mr. and Mrs.

Blakesley getting to know one another and eventually marrying. It was just like Fritz to put himself out in such a way to help a friend. There were few men who were more compassionate than he.

"It was not very well done on my part," Mrs. Blakesley continued with a peek over her shoulder to where her husband walked with Aunt Augusta. "If I had known of his past, I would have never asked him to help me," she whispered.

"His past?"

Mrs. Blakesley nodded and peeked over her shoulder once again as if she did not want the others to know of what she was speaking.

"My husband told me about you," she whispered. "I do not say this to make you uneasy, though I suspect it will." She sighed as if she did not wish to say what she was about to say but had no option but to say it. "I asked Mr. Norman to play the part of my beau because I knew that neither my sister nor my mother would approve of my being courted by a physician."

Belle sucked in a quick breath. How difficult that must have been for Fritz!

"That is exactly how I felt when I discovered

what had happened in his past. I can assure you that I have asked his forgiveness, but he assures me there is nothing to forgive. He knew the part he was playing. He is such a dear friend. However, I still feel dreadful about it all."

"That is understandable," Belle assured her, "but how were you to know about what had happened to him without being told?"

"It does not matter if I knew or not," Mrs. Blakesley protested firmly. "I should not have done it, for I was only thinking of myself."

"What do you mean you were only thinking of yourself? Were you not keeping your relationship with Mr. Blakesley a secret because your sister likes to flirt?" That was what she had been told, was it not? And she sincerely doubted that Mrs. Blakesley would lie to her about such a thing.

"Oh, it was most certainly because of that, for Felicity had stolen two very good gentlemen from me. Well, stole is perhaps not the best word as that would imply I had secured those gentlemen. I had not, for I was not given an opportunity to even attempt to secure either one of them since Felicity was the eldest."

"I think you could say that she stole two prospects from you then."

"Yes, that is it precisely."

"And because of that, you feared she would ruin your chance with Mr. Blakesley, did you not?"

"I was dreadfully afraid, and I thought only about keeping her from discovering him instead of considering how what I was asking might affect anyone save me."

Ah, that was what she had meant. Belle was not certain that such a thing was so selfish as Mrs. Blakesley thought it was, for to Belle it seemed prudent.

Mrs. Blakesley wrapped her arm more tightly around Belle's. "However, as it turns out," she whispered, "Felicity would not have been successful with Walter."

There was a very pleased and amused tone to Mrs. Blakesley's voice as she peeked once more toward her husband. Belle could not help but envy the open adoration that both Mrs. and Mr. Blakesley showed for each other. Her admiration for the man she loved would always have to remain hidden until such time as she could purge it from her heart.

"In the end, I was extremely fortunate not to have gained the notice of one particular gentleman whom Felicity had secured, and I am dreadfully sorry my sister was successful."

The sad tone from earlier when Mrs. Blakesley had spoken of her home was back.

"If it is not too much of an intrusion, may I ask why that is?"

Mrs. Blakesley drew in a deep breath and let it out with a grieved sigh. "If I tell you, it must be kept in the strictest confidence."

"I am not a gossip, for I know how damaging it can be."

"That is right. You are intimately acquainted with the grief a tale might bring." She paused. "My sister was foolish and, after having been promised an offer of marriage, allowed this gentleman liberties that he should have only received from his wife."

"Oh." That was shocking.

"Indeed. I am waiting to hear if I will be an aunt or not. And the worst part of it all is that he abandoned her."

"Dear me, that is horrible." The sadness in the

way Mrs. Blakesley spoke of her home made perfect sense now.

"It is."

"This gentleman could not be made to marry your sister?"

Mrs. Blakesley shook her head. "No one knows where he is. He just disappeared into the night."

Belle's heart sank. She knew all-too-well that there were individuals in the world who did not care for anything beyond themselves. Her father was that way in some things, and her brother Andrew had been as well. They had not cared one bit about what happened to Fritz so long as he did not marry her. According to them, Belle was too rich and beautiful to be wasted on a poor physician, who had no significant connections to offer her father.

"Walter tried to find him, but not for Felicity's sake, for mine."

"You have been fortunate to find such a gentleman to love you." Very, very fortunate.

"I am fortunate, am I not?"

"Yes, you are." How she longed to have such good fortune shine on her.

"And what about you?" Mrs. Blakesley asked.

"You could be so blessed. Mr. Norman is a very dear man."

Tears sprang unbidden to Belle's eyes, causing her to blink rapidly to dispel them. "That can never be," she said softly.

"Are you certain?"

Belle swallowed against the lump of sorrow that rose in her throat. "Yes."

Any hope she had harbored in the deepest recesses of her heart had flown out the door with Fritz today. He could not even stay in a room with her. He obviously did not want her.

"Do you love him or did you?"

Belle nodded. "I did, but it can never be."

"Are you absolutely sure you do not wish to attempt to persuade him to consider you?"

"Yes." Oh, how she would love to do just that! But, it was not possible.

"Then, I shall cross your name off my list. I had it at the top."

Belle blinked. "Your list? What list?"

"Why, of possible Mrs. Normans, of course," Mrs. Blakesley replied rather cheerfully. "I thought helping him find a wife was the least I could do to repay him for his help in my securing Walter."

The world tipped in a most nauseating fashion. Belle's hand rested on her chest. She could still feel a heartbeat – a strong and rapid one. She was not dying if her heart was beating, although she felt as though she might expire.

"You are going to find him a wife?" The words seemed to scrape and scratch her throat as she forced them out.

"I am." Mrs. Blakesley's brow furrowed. "Are you well? You do not look well." She pulled Belle toward the benches at the end of the garden. "Shall I call my husband to send for the physi — Oh, that would not do, would it?"

Belle shook her head. She must not swoon or ever become ill.

"Does he wish to marry?" she asked Mrs. Blakesley.

Had he truly forgotten her? Was a gentleman's love so much frailer than a lady's? She could not even entertain the idea of loving another.

"I believe he does." Mrs. Blakesley was looking at her warily. "He agreed to allow me to assist him – though I must admit his agreement was not readily given."

"Are you in need of assistance?"

Wonderful! Mr. Blakesley had noticed her indisposition.

"I need only a moment to rest," Belle assured him.

"Are you unwell?" Aunt Augusta asked.

"No, no. I am well."

"You do not look it. I can send someone to find Mr. Norman."

"No!" Belle cried. "I promise you I was only momentarily startled."

"By what were you startled, Miss Chapman?" Mr. Blakesley directed the question to her, but his eyes were on his wife.

"It was my fault." Mrs. Blakesley pulled a trembling lower lip between her teeth.

"You are not at fault. I just was not prepared to think about Mr. Norman marrying." Belle turned pleading eyes to Mr. Blakesley. "Please do not be angry with her. It truly was not her doing."

Mr. Blakesley arched a brow. "I am not angry. I am concerned. What did you say, Grace?" He handed his handkerchief to his wife to dry the tears that threatened.

"I asked her if she was set against Mr. Norman – not in those words, but that is the essence of our conversation." She squeezed her eyes shut. "Then, I mentioned my offer to help Mr. Norman find a wife."

"You are set against him?" There was no little amount of surprised displeasure in Aunt Augusta's tone.

"Yes."

Her aunt lifted her chin and looked not altogether pleased. "Then, you will not mind if I make a few suggestions about other possible matches?"

Belle opened her mouth to say no but then closed it again. She could not declare that she would not marry anyone but Fritz without having to detail why she was set against him when she, in reality, longed for him and only him. Or could she?

"As I have told my mother and my father, I have no notion of marrying, for I think I should be able to be quite content as the mistress of my own domain just as you are. However, if you wish to suggest a few possible matches for me, I will not stop you." She smiled as her aunt's eyes narrowed. It was not the answer she had attempted to provoke from Belle. "And, in return, I am certain that you, Aunt, would not mind my making a few suggestions for you."

"Suggestions for me?" her aunt gasped.

"I will not suggest anyone who is gouty or whose ears and eyes are clouded by the ravages of time. I know how you like the best." Teasing her aunt was a delightful way to pull herself out of her morose of a moment ago. It was also, she hoped, a grand way to keep her aunt from parading too many gentlemen before her.

Her aunt held her gaze for a half minute, searching for something, before sighing. Whether she had found what she sought or not, Belle did not know, but either way, Aunt Augusta seemed resigned.

"Very well. You may point out gentlemen to me, and I shall do the same for you while Mrs. Blakesley assists Mr. Norman in finding a wife." Her aunt's left eyebrow rose just a trifle when, despite her best efforts, Belle flinched at the mention of a future Mrs. Norman.

"I might have the names of an older gentleman or two which I could share with you, Miss Chapman, since you are new in town and not acquainted with too many." Mr. Blakesley smiled broadly. "I would not want your aunt to have an unfair advantage."

"Well," Aunt Augusta said with a huff.

"It seems only proper that I repay you for your service in attempting to match me with several young ladies."

Aunt Augusta chuckled. "I have no intention of marrying again, but you may both try your best. It will give me a reason to acquire a new dress or two." She winked at Belle.

"I do not need any new dresses," Belle replied to her aunt's unspoken suggestion.

"Yes, you do."

"No, I do not."

"Ah, but think of the fun we shall have shopping. And Mrs. Blakesley can join us if her husband will allow it." She cocked an eyebrow in challenge at Mr. Blakesley.

"Three," the man answered smugly.

"Three new dresses?" Mrs. Blakesley cried.

"Yes, I do believe that is the number of dresses which had been intended for you but were given to your sister. Is it not?"

"It is!" Mrs. Blakesley turned to Belle to explain. "My sister was here for her season after throwing over a gentleman she had nearly promised to marry, and, with such a blemish on her reputation, I was required to give up my season so that she would have the best advantage of making a match."

"Oh." Once again, Mrs. Blakesley's sister left Belle at a loss for words. It seemed that, though the circumstances were not exactly the same, she and Mrs. Blakesley had something in common – appalling relations.

"Three seems a perfect number," Aunt Augusta declared. "We will have to plan an outing to the shops."

Her aunt looked perfectly delighted by this turn of events.

"Tell me, Mrs. Blakesley, what were the dresses like which you gave up." Aunt Augusta held out her hand to Grace and, once the lady was on her feet, drew her along the path back to the house.

"My wife means well," Mr. Blakesley said as he offered Belle his arm.

"I like her very much."

"I cannot imagine anyone not liking her."

Belle could not help but smile at the sweetness of the comment. "You know, neither can I, Mr. Blakesley, neither can I."

Chapter 7

Three days later, a rather fidgety Fritz patted his cravat. It felt as if it was in place and as it should be. Then, he straightened the sleeves of his coat. Satisfied that he was presentable, he stepped into the ballroom and began a circuit to his left. If he reached the card room before he saw either Miss James or Miss Wesley, he would cross over to the tearoom and procure a bit of tea before presenting himself to any other young ladies.

He was oddly on edge tonight compared to any other night when he had been here, but then, again, he had never been here attempting to find a replacement for Belle while she was watching.

Guilt clawed at his mind. It felt wrong, dreadfully wrong, to be thinking of anyone as a future bride when Belle was present. It had been much easier to subdue such thoughts when he was imagining her contentedly settled into life as someone's wife. Not that imagining her with someone else had ever been pleasant. It had just made it easier for him to search for a bride who was not her.

But, she had not married. He wondered if she had just never found anyone to offer for her – an excessively unlikely thing for she was beautiful – or if her father had never found a gentleman with a fine enough pedigree to allow her to marry.

"Norman."

Fritz nodded a greeting to Walter, who was no doubt just waiting for the music to begin so that he could lead his wife out for the first set.

That wife leaned closer to her husband and whispered to Fritz. "I have picked out two very pretty ladies to add to our list. However, I have not yet had a chance to meet them. Are your ladies here? I should very much like to form an opinion about them."

Fritz had told Mrs. Blakesley about the two young ladies, whom he had learned about at the Pump Room, when he had dined with the Blakesleys on the evening of that very day three days ago.

"I was just looking for them. I know Miss James by sight, but I have yet to meet Miss Wesley. She just arrived at her grandfather's home last evening, and I was not able to stay for a cup of tea today as planned after Mr. Wesley's appointment."

His eyes scanned the room, searching for Miss Philips or Mr. Wesley. There. There was Miss Philips. Now, where was her niece? "Ah, there is Miss James."

"Where?" Mrs. Blakesley asked eagerly.

"Do you see the two ladies on the left near the door?"

"There are at least twenty ladies near the door," Walter answered.

"Yes, but these two have a younger lady with them. She has light brown hair and is wearing a lavender dress."

"Oh! I think I see her." Mrs. Blakesley tipped her head and furrowed her brow. "She looks very pretty from here. Do you think we could meet her?" She directed this question to her husband.

"If Norman will introduce us, I suppose we might."

"Will that not seem as if I am giving her more

notice than I ought?" Fritz's heart thumped in his ears as his palms grew damp.

"You will have to declare yourself at some point," Walter answered.

"Must it be now?" He rubbed his hands together, which was the most foolish thing to do. How was one sweaty hand supposed to dry another? It was as if his intellect had stayed at home tonight.

"I guess we could wait," Mrs. Blakesley said.

The disappointment in Mrs. Blakesley's tone could not overcome the relief Fritz felt at putting off his need to make any significant public statement about his intentions toward Miss James.

"Thank you. I will go secure a set, and then, later, perhaps, I can introduce her to you." He accepted Mrs. Blakesley's "very well" before directing his feet to cross the room.

"Miss Philips, Mrs. James, Miss James," he said with a bow for the ladies. "I was wondering if Miss James was engaged for the first set or if she might be free so that I could claim it."

"She is very free," Miss Philips said with great excitement. "Very free, indeed. This is her first ball while in Bath, you see. Therefore, she has not yet had a great deal of time to meet very many gentlemen. There are two others who we hope will present themselves tonight, but I must say I am delighted, absolutely delighted, that you were first." She lowered her voice. "You are, to my way of thinking, the best of the three, but that is not for me to decide, now is it?"

"No, Aunt, it is not," Miss James said. "However, I would be pleased to accept your hand for the first set, Mr. Norman."

There. It was done. He had secured one dance as he had promised to do when he had met Miss James three days ago. However, there were still a few minutes before the music would begin. He looked to his left and then his right as he wondered where Mr. Wesley and his granddaughter might be.

"It was a beautiful day today, despite the rain," Mrs. James said. "We made use of our umbrellas and took a nice walk."

"I am happy to hear it. Did you walk far?"

"No, not overly so. I did not wish for Margaret to be too tired to enjoy tonight's dancing." Mrs. James looked fondly at her daughter. "Not that Margaret has a weak constitution. It is as strong as they come. She has rarely had more than a sniffle, and then, that has only lasted a day or two at most."

"That is a blessing."

"She takes prodigious good care of herself," Miss Philips said. "She is not one to scoff at sound advice. In that way we are similar, are we not, Margaret?"

"Yes, Aunt." A smile played at Miss James's mouth.

"Do you also question the advice you are given as your aunt does, Miss James?" Mr. Norman asked.

Miss Philips tittered.

"I am afraid I do." Miss James's eyes danced with merriment.

"I told you we were much alike," Miss Philips reminded him.

"You did, indeed, tell me that."

"And yet, you agreed to meet me?"

It seemed that Miss James possessed a wry, teasing sense of humour that reminded him of Belle. It was a trait that he found quite pleasant.

"If I know my sister, as I think I do," Mrs. James said, "she likely gave you no choice but to meet Margaret. I freely admit to doting on my daughter and likely give her too much freedom, but it is nothing compared to how her aunt spoils her."

Again, Fritz thought of Belle. This time,

however, it was not to compare how she and Miss James were alike, but rather of how, unlike Miss James, Belle had been given very little freedom. Either her father or brother was always present, making certain that she was not soiling herself with the common people such as him. However, from what he could tell, she would be very happy with her aunt, for Mrs. King was a kind woman who seemed to adore her niece, just as Miss Philips adored Miss James.

The instruments, which had been filling the room with squeaks and squawks as they prepared to perform, fell silent.

"I believe that is our cue to take the floor." He offered his arm to Miss James and led her out to stand next to Mrs. Blakesley. This would be a natural way for the two to meet without the introductions being seen as more than a happy coincidence. "Miss James. May I introduce you to some friends while we wait to begin?"

"You will have to do it quickly," she replied with a smile.

"I shall be as quick as can be," he assured her. "Miss James, the gentleman at my side," he motioned to Walter, "is my dearest friend, Mr.

Blakesley, and across from him and on your left, is his wife, Mrs. Blakesley. Blakesley, Mrs. Blakesley, this is Miss Philips's niece, Miss James."

"Who is Miss Philips?" Mrs. Blakesley asked.

Oh, he had forgotten that, though Walter knew who Miss Philips was, his wife would not.

"She is my aunt who my mother and I are visiting."

"You are not from Bath then?"

"No, we are not from Bath, but our home is not overly far from here as it is near Taunton. It is not even a full day's drive."

"How pleasant for you! I was from Kent," Mrs. Blakesley replied, "but I am from Bath now. It is a lovely town, do you not think?"

"What I have seen of it is most agreeable."

"Have you seen a great deal?"

"No, some shops and the Pump Room is the extent of my knowledge of Bath."

"You shall have to go to the Sydney Gardens. It is such a prodigiously good place to take some exercise. I find a walk in the park to be just the thing to relax and refresh one's spirits."

"I will keep that in mind," Miss James said as the first notes of a reel were played.

"Mr. Norman's home is not far from there," Mrs. Blakesley added before she was required to join hands with her husband and cross to the other line, where she joined hands with Fritz to complete two circles. "She seems very nice."

"Yes, she does," Fritz agreed.

Miss James seemed to be all that was pleasant. She had a lively humour, yet, she comported herself with a calmness that belied her youth. He really would not mind getting to know her better. She also danced very well. She was just as light on her feet as Belle had ever been, and she seemed to enjoy the activity immensely, which was good since Fritz relished a dance and the way it made his blood course through his body at a rapid pace.

For the next several minutes, Fritz enjoyed the weaving and circling of the dance as he watched Miss James complete the patterns with a word here and there passing between her and Mrs. Blakesley when possible. They seemed to be forming a fine acquaintance. This was also a good thing as Fritz could not countenance taking a wife who might separate him from Walter.

Walter had been the first close acquaintance that Fritz had made in Bath. Fritz had been here for two years, establishing himself as a physician before he had met Walter when Walter had fallen ill with a fever. It had not been a serious illness, just enough of one to require some advice for regaining health. The meeting had been as much of a balm to Fritz's soul as his tinctures and recipe for barley water had been to Walter.

Walter had healed quickly, and then, he had provided his own sort of healing to Fritz. It was Walter who had taught him that there were still people in the world who were trustworthy and loyal and who were opposed to carrying tales and viewing themselves as better than everyone else. They had been fast friends ever since. Fritz could not give up such a relationship. He simply could not. Therefore, he was excessively pleased when upon the completion of their set of dances, Miss James invited the Blakesleys to meet her mother and aunt.

Miss James was a very good candidate as a possible future Mrs. Norman. He would have to make certain that Mrs. Blakesley kept Miss James's name at the top of the list.

"Ah, Mr. Norman," Mr. Wesley greeted him as he approached the place where Miss Philips and

Mrs. James stood. "You have not forgotten about my Charlotte, have you?"

"We shall not keep him from you," Miss Philips said. "We are agreed that he will be allowed time to get to know both of our favourite young ladies and then make a decision."

Fritz sighed.

"He is a fine catch," Walter teased.

"Oh, indeed, he is!" Mrs. Blakesley agreed.

"We thought he was going to claim you at one time," Mr. Wesley said. "But, who can blame you for picking Blakesley over Norman."

Mrs. Blakesley looked aghast. "Oh, I was not choosing one over the other. I... I..." She looked at Fritz and shrugged while wearing a look of bewilderment which said she did not know how to explain herself.

"I have already told them that we were only good friends," Fritz assured her.

"Yes, yes, that is it." Relief washed over her features.

"Did you not sigh over him?" Miss Philips asked. "I am certain I heard you had."

"It was to torment her mother," Fritz offered. "You know how some relations can be in pushing forward those about whom they care." He held Mr. Wesley's gaze for a moment before shifting his focus to Miss Philips. "Now, if you will kindly allow Blakesley to introduce his wife to you."

"Thank you, Norman. There is no better friend in all of Bath to help a fellow win a wife as Norman has done for me. And isn't she a pretty thing?" He winked at Mr. Wesley as his wife blushed and smiled. "Grace, my dear," he continued, "this is Mr. Wesley, and this is Miss Philips. I have known both for several years now. Miss Philips and Mr. Wesley, this is the pretty lady who has stolen my heart and made me the happiest of men."

"Oh, it is a delight to meet you, Mrs. Blakesley. You have always seemed so charming when I have seen you. I can see why Mr. Blakesley is so smitten," Miss Philips said.

"Thank you."

"And this is my sister, Mrs. James, Margaret's mother," Miss Philips added.

"A pleasure, ma'am," Blakesley said with a bow of his head.

"You must meet my wife and granddaughter," Mr. Wesley inserted. "They are just down the line a pace."

"We should like to meet your granddaughter as well," Miss Philips said as Mr. Wesley began to lead Fritz and the Blakesleys away.

"Yes, yes. I shall introduce you, but not until after Mr. Norman has danced with Charlotte."

"That man," Miss Philips muttered.

"It seems you are a prize which is highly sought after," Walter whispered to Fritz.

"So it would seem."

"And why should he not be?" Mrs. Blakesley asked.

"I am a physician," Fritz replied.

"The best in Bath I hear," she retorted with a grin. "You are highly respected and well-established. Any sensible person would think you a great match for their daughter or sister or niece or whomever." She pulled her lower lip between her teeth as her eyes held some sorrow. "Unfortunately, my mother is not so sensible as she should be."

"I knew what I was about," Fritz reminded her. How many times was she going to apologize to him for that?

"I, for one, am quite glad your mother is not

more sensible." Walter winked at Norman. "For it worked very well in my favour."

Mrs. Blakesley smiled at her husband. It was that secret sort of smile she saved just for him. Fritz had never seen her use it with anyone else. Maybe one day, he would have a lady who would look at him in such a fashion – if that were even possible since he was not marrying for love as much as he was for convenience. Maybe it would be Miss James, or...

He bowed to the petite blonde being presented to him. "Miss Wesley, it is a pleasure to finally meet you."

Chapter 8

While the dance set which was about to commence was the third set of the night, for Belle, it was the first set she would dance.

During the first set of dances, Aunt Augusta had spoken with Mrs. Newnham, the wife of the master of ceremonies. Belle had attempted to pay attention to what was being said between the two women, but she had not been so successful as she had hoped to be, for she had seen Fritz take the floor with a pretty young lady. He was still as light on his feet as he had always been, and his partner had done him great justice with her mastery of the figures.

Instead of attending to Mrs. Newnham's tale about a new table she had just received, Belle had tortured herself with thoughts of Fritz and his dance partner marrying. She had done it purposefully to assist herself in hardening her heart to the idea. She would not again be taken by surprise as she had been in her aunt's garden when Mrs. Blakesley had told her about assisting Fritz in finding a wife. She would find her resolve and paint a pleased smile on her face rather than allowing her heart to etch her features with what it was truly feeling.

Thankfully, during the second set of dances, Belle had only had time to see Fritz escort another pretty lady into formation before her aunt and Mrs. Newnham had drawn her away to be presented to those gentlemen of higher rank who were in attendance. These were gentlemen who would appreciate the fact that she was a baronet's daughter and who would be considered worthy candidates for her hand by her father.

This was how she had come to be standing across from Mr. Doherty as the third set of dances began. In silence, she and her partner wove their way through the first several steps of the dance.

"For someone who claims not to like dancing, Mr. Doherty, you perform admirably."

It seemed silly to not at least have a few words of conversation with a gentleman she was supposed to consider as a possible suitor. One could not determine anything of significance from watching someone perform a set of patterns. Inspection of a person's character and intellect was best done through a combination of observance of actions and contemplation of words.

"Disliking something does not equate to a lack of capability." He turned from her, wove his way in and out, and rejoined her.

"If you despise the activity so much, why do you punish yourself by attending balls?" she asked.

Mr. Doherty truly did not look as if he was enjoying himself in any way. The corners of his mouth were turned down the tiniest bit, and his eyes lacked any sort of sparkle. There was no trace of enjoyment in either his features or his frame. He was performing a dance, but he was not truly dancing, for dancing, in Belle's way of thinking, came from the soul, pouring out a dancer's delight as he absorbed and then expressed the music in his movements. That was how Fritz danced – as if he were part of the rhythm and melody of the song. Mr. Doherty, for all his thousands of pounds upon which Mrs. Newnham had based her recommendation of him as a suitable match, could not compare to Fritz as a dance partner.

"It is a place to find a wife."

Mr. Doherty's answer was rather bluntly truthful, but Belle appreciated his honesty.

"I should think that you would not wish for a wife who liked dancing, sir. For would that not mean a lifetime of participating in that which you despise?"

"I wish for a wife who possesses both elegance and grace." His lips actually curled into a small smile. It was the first time he had looked anything but grave since Belle had met him, and she had to admit that, even though it was only a mildly pleasant expression, it added greatly to his handsomeness. "A lady who skips lightly through a dance is in possession of a good dose of both of those things."

That did make sense. Again, she found herself appreciating his direct answers and added to that an admiration of his ability to reason logically.

"See that lady there? The one there with the green sash on her dress." He indicated the lady in the group of dancers next to them with a tip of his head. "She has stumbled three times already.

Therefore, I shall not be asking for an introduction, even though I know her to have a great fortune and good connections."

That was harsh! To dismiss a lady completely based on a few missteps? Perhaps her admiration of his way of thinking and directness had been premature, for it seemed now to be nothing more than an arrogant gentleman, refusing to give any more of his time and attention to his partner than was absolutely necessary to give a response. His ability to conduct a conversation was much like his dancing. He was performing the steps, but he was not pouring himself into the activity.

"Could she not just be having a poor night? Those three stumbles might be the only ones she has ever made while dancing. Are you not being hasty in your judgment?"

He shook his head. "There are so many ladies to assess. One must have some criteria for acceptance or refusal."

To Belle, it seemed that Mr. Doherty had the perfect amount of arrogance to delight her father. She nearly shuddered at the thought as she joined hands with the man.

"You have a sister, do you not?" She would press

her point with him for she needed to know if his arrogance was as deeply rooted as her father's was.

His eyes narrowed. "I do." Suspicion suffused both his mien and his tone.

"My aunt pointed you out in the gardens the other day. I assure you that I have not been seeking information about you."

He did not look convinced.

"You appeared to be fond of her."

"I am." His response seemed unwillingly given, which was a change from his ready answers of a moment ago.

"What if she was passed over as a possible match by someone based on one poor dance?"

He chuckled in a fashion that said such a question was ridiculous. "Why a gentleman who would do such a thing would not be good enough for her, of course, and it would save me the trouble of refusing him."

Belle smiled. "Then, some fellow here tonight should be grateful."

He blinked. "I do not have the pleasure of understanding your meaning. Which fellow?"

She shrugged as she took her place and curtseyed as the first dance of their set ended.

"Why the fellow who will not have to refuse you for being unworthy of his sister, of course."

His eyes grew wide, and his nostrils flared. She had struck a chord as she thought she might. Her father never liked being told he was not universally adored, and it seemed Mr. Doherty shared that same trait. However, he spoke not a word, which was exactly the opposite of what her father would do. Sir Allen would sputter and gape before proclaiming any person, who dared to disparage him, a fool and not worthy of his attention.

The second dance of their set began and was several measures into its progression before Mr. Doherty finally spoke. "Your point was valid."

Four words. And then a return to silence for several more measures of music.

"I will be certain to seek her out at the next ball and see if she stumbles there."

"That is generous of you. Of course, from the way she is smiling at her partner, I dare say you would have a difficult time winning her over."

Once again, Mr. Doherty looked startled. "Indeed? Has she been smiling at him?"

"Yes, very brightly. I should think just from my observation of her interactions that she is quite taken with him and that theirs is not a first meeting. They seem very familiar."

"Do they?" He turned his head to look at the couple and stumbled in the process.

"Oh, Mr. Doherty," Belle said with a smile, "I am afraid you have only two mishaps left before I must cast you aside."

This comment produced a reaction that Belle had not expected. She had thought that Mr. Doherty would become flustered and put out. However, his response was quite the opposite. A smile suffused his features, and he chuckled in a most agreeable fashion.

"You have made your point very clearly," he said as they came to the final steps of the dance. "I will remember your words and attempt to judge less harshly."

If he had not just smiled and chuckled at her comment, she would have doubted his sincerity, but as it was, she decided to accept his words as true. Perhaps his arrogance was not so entrenched as her father's was. Maybe the true Mr. Doherty lay hidden behind a façade of arrogance. The thought intrigued her.

"I thank you for the dance," she said as she

placed her hand in his to be led back to where her aunt stood.

"And I thank you. It was most pleasant." He bowed and left her with her aunt.

"What did you think?" Aunt Augusta whispered behind her fan. "He is very handsome, and you looked very well together. Not that I am one to form my opinions on the superficial."

"He has potential."

If he could be more relaxed as he had been at the end of their set, Mr. Doherty might be an agreeable suitor. She had behaved with him as she always had with Fritz, and he had not dismissed her. That was a mark in his favour, though he still had a fair distance to go before he came close to making her feel as welcomed and at home as Fritz always had.

She sighed. There was not another like Fritz, and she must accept that fact. That was why she truly was not in favour of contemplating suitors and husbands. None could ever replace Fritz.

"What is that sigh?" Aunt Augusta asked. "Do you not approve of him?"

Belle shook her head. "It is just... well... it does not signify."

"Are you certain?" Aunt August looked at her with no little amount of concern in her eyes.

"Yes. It is merely that my thoughts are tangled and in a need of sorting."

"If you are certain."

"I am," she replied with a small smile.

Thankfully, her aunt did not press the point.

"Miss Chapman?" Mr. Baily stood before them. "Are you engaged for this dance?"

Mr. Baily, whom she had danced with at a previous assembly, was an amiable gentleman. To dance with him would be no chore.

"No, I am not." She willingly extended her hand to him.

"Did you enjoy the rain today?" Mr. Baily asked.

"It was not completely intolerable."

"Very good." The words were spoken true delight as if her being not put out by the rain was the most wonderful thing in the world. "I find it is best to be able to enjoy all sorts of weather but especially rain as there is so much of it, it seems." He looked to where the musicians were seated with eager anticipation.

Mr. Baily clearly enjoyed dancing, and she had to admit that, though she had only spoken to him during one set of dances before tonight, he made her feel as if she was in the presence of an old friend. With a curtsy, she happily began the first dance of their set, assured that it would be a very enjoyable half-hour.

~*~*~

As a clock chimed eleven, signalling the end to the dancing, Belle had to admit that the evening had been invigorating. She had not wanted for a partner for any dance, for once she had been returned to her aunt and before her aunt had been allowed more than a brief interrogation about whichever gentleman had been her partner, another arrived to claim a dance. She had not had so much attention since her first season in London. It was a pleasant feeling to be so sought after – especially at her age — and it filled her with a sense of contentment she had not expected to feel tonight after dancing in the same room as Fritz without ever once speaking to him.

"Did you enjoy yourself?" Her aunt asked as they strolled arm in arm from the ballroom and towards the hall which led to where their carriage would be waiting.

"I did. I truly did." In fact, it was nearly a perfect evening.

Looking back toward the ballroom, she saw Fritz speaking to the first lady he had danced with tonight. Yes, the night had been nearly perfect, but perfection was never again to be. Swallowing her sorrow at the thought, she turned her head away from Fritz and, with determined steps, allowed her aunt to escort her from the Upper Rooms and into the possibility of an almost perfect future.

Chapter 9

Fritz grasped his walking stick firmly, as if attempting to squeeze the polished wood into a different form would somehow keep him from being part of the scene in which he found himself. Miss James was babbling on and on about how a particular dress, which was her favourite, had been nearly ruined by a carriage passing too quickly and mud splattering her in the process.

"I was never more startled," she concluded.

Babbling was perhaps not a fair assessment, Fritz chided himself. She had been merely attempting to conduct a conversation.

"That seems logical," he murmured to fill the void of silence which followed her words.

"I say, is not Mr. Doherty looking all that is handsome today?"

Fritz blinked and turned towards her. "Mr. Doherty?"

"The gentleman there." She discreetly pointed in the direction of a well-dressed fellow who had just entered the pump room.

"I know who he is." Fritz knew very well who that blasted man was. He was one of the two gentlemen who seemed to be frequently at Belle's side. With any luck, Doherty might run Baily off, and Fritz would no longer need to stare daggers at him as he strolled with Belle.

"Would you introduce me? I have not met him and would very much like to. I hear he holds more hot air in his little finger than a southerly gale in the summer, but he is very handsome, do you not think?"

Fritz stopped walking. "You wish for *me* to introduce *you* to another gentleman?" Was that not the opposite of what a lady should expect from him when he had specifically requested to walk with that lady?

Miss James smiled sadly at him. "Does it not seem logical?" she asked.

Logical? Why would introducing the lady whom you were attempting to half-heartedly court to another potential suitor – one who was far more handsome and wealthy – be logical?

"I apologize, but I do not understand your meaning."

"*That seems logical* has been your reply to nearly everything I have said since you joined me for a walk."

Understanding dawned with great force. "Has it truly been all I have said?"

She nodded. "You seem rather distracted."

He was. He very much was, and he had been so ever since the ball at the assembly rooms a week and a half ago. Seeing Belle dancing with so many gentlemen of wealth and rank had been much harder than he had imagined it would be. And now, here she was, taking a turn of the pump room, with one of those gentlemen with whom she had danced. How could he not be distracted?

"I apologize."

"Would you care to tell me what is occupying your mind so much that you cannot attend to a conversation today?"

No, he did not want to do that!

"It is a dreadful habit," he lied. "I often find myself lost in contemplation." There was some truth in that statement. He did often allow himself to become immersed in his thoughts. Of course, that was usually when he was alone, and almost never when he was in company. His ears warmed.

"Hmm. Is that so?" was all that Miss James replied in words but her raised eyebrows and her tone assured him that she did not believe his explanation. But then, her aunt had said she was the skeptical sort, so perhaps this was her natural response to many things. At least, he could hope it was.

"Do you truly wish for an introduction? Mr. Doherty and I are not very well acquainted as I am not one of his sphere."

Her lips pursed and her eyes danced with amusement. "No. I do not care for gentlemen who hold themselves so far above others. See how his chin is never level with the horizon but is always above it? Such a gentleman thinks too well of himself." She lowered her voice as the object of her observations drew near. "He is handsome, but not pleasant enough to tempt me. I much prefer a kinder sort of gentleman." She ducked her head. "Such as yourself."

"When I am not distracted."

"Yes."

"I shall attempt to put my contemplations aside for now."

"Are you certain you do not wish to discuss them? I am no stranger to unsettling details of illness and injury. As you know, I have a brother who was injured on the continent. I have heard many disturbing tales, and I saw his wounds when sitting with him once he was returned home to us."

Fritz knew that about her. It was one of the things which recommended her to him. She did not seem to be the squeamish sort. Miss Wesley, who was a lovely and sober young lady and who was presently walking on the arm of her grandfather, appeared to be more given to fits of the vapours than Miss James ever would be. That was why Fritz had singled out Miss James as the lady with the greatest chance of filling the role of a physician's wife best. Not that she would ever fill it as well as Belle would. His eyes stole a look in that particular lady's direction.

"I assure you I am capable of hearing whatever you have to say," Miss James prompted him again.

"It is a personal matter. I shall not bore you with the details." That was as truthful as he was going to get about what was plaguing him. He had to give Belle up. He must.

"I think I should like to return to my aunt now." The statement was soft and sad.

"Was I doing it again?" he asked as shame filled him. He was not usually the sort of fellow who offended others, and that fact that he had done so more than once made him feel dreadful.

She nodded. "You did not hear a word I said about understanding that some things are more challenging to share than other things."

"Allow me to apologize once again." His eyes searched her forlorn ones. "It is not that I do not find you interesting and a wonderful companion. It is just that I..." How did one say this?

"It is just that we do not suit," Miss James supplied. "I had hoped for my aunt's sake that we would, but we do not."

She was sending him away. He had not thought that would happen, but at present, he also could not fault her for doing so. He had been inattentive and not at all charming.

"I am truly sorry that we do not." It was the most honest thing he had likely said all day. He had enjoyed walking with her, dancing with her, and taking tea with her. It had all been very pleasant and friendly. "Would it be possible to remain friends?"

Her expression relaxed and a small smile formed on her lips. "I believe that is possible. It seems more like what we were destined to be."

"Does it?"

She nodded as she took his arm again, and they began the walk back to where her aunt and mother were waiting.

"I had hoped it might become more. You are a wonderful man. My aunt speaks so highly of you, and not without reason. I can see that she is right, but to be honest, if I cannot hold your attention for the length of a walk, then I think anything further than a friendship would be doomed before it began. I fear I am a very practical sort of person in that way. I do not see a reason to pursue something that is not there." She chuckled softly. "This is why I am in danger of becoming a spinster. Just ask my mother. She thinks I give up too easily."

Fritz shook his head. "You just want your heart to be stirred so greatly that your head has no choice but to follow."

"Yes!" she cried in delight. "That is precisely it."

"It is the same for me, though I fear my heart was lost a long time ago, and as much as I would like to have a family and children of my own to worry over, I doubt it will ever be."

"How sad! Are you sure you would not like to tell me about it?"

"It is best left where it is."

She tipped her head and smiled. "Well, should you ever decide you need to talk to someone about it, I am as good at listening as I am at talking." She laughed. "My aunt and I are a lot alike in that way."

He joined her in a chuckle. "You do not lack talent in holding up your part of the conversation. I, on the other hand..."

"Could use some practice," she concluded.

"Indeed!" he agreed.

"You look as if you are getting along very well," Miss Philip said when they had joined her.

"As good friends should," Miss James said, causing her mother to groan.

"You did not," Mrs. James said.

"I am afraid I did. Mr. Norman is a perfect gentleman and will make someone a marvelous husband someday. However, it will not be me. We have agreed that we shall remain friends and naught else."

"I do apologize," Mrs. James said to Fritz. "She has such strange notions about marriage." The last part was said in nearly a whisper and with a blush.

"They are not strange at all," Fritz said. "I find her ideas to be perfect."

"But is it possible?" her mother asked.

"For some." He could just see Belle out of the corner of his eye. Was it possible for him? Would he ever again be led by his heart toward happiness?

"I will not lie," Miss Philips said. "I am disappointed. I quite liked the thought of claiming you as a relation."

"In all honesty, Miss Philips, I liked the idea of someone wishing for me to be their relation. It has not always been so." It had been a novel and excessively pleasing feeling to be wanted in such a fashion.

"There are plenty of fools in this world," Miss Philips replied. "Why once when I was young – which was not so very many years ago as one might think –"

"Aunt," Miss James interrupted.

"It is an applicable story," her aunt retorted.

"I think Mr. Norman would like to be on his way. I have disappointed him after all." She smiled at him.

Miss Philips looked stricken. "You will still call on me, will you not? Even if my niece has been the cause of a disappointment?"

"Of course. I am not so disappointed as I thought I might be, which," he glanced at Mrs. James and then returned his attention to Miss Philips, "proves that Miss James's decision was a wise one." He bowed. "I wish you well, and I will see you again soon. I promise."

Miss Philips sighed audibly. "That is good." She turned to her sister and niece as he was walking away. "There is no one better than Mr. Norman. Are you certain you are set against the match?"

He chuckled to himself. This was a new experience. There was a relation of a pretty and intelligent young lady who thought it a travesty that she would not consider him as a husband. It was the exact opposite of what had transpired six years ago. He stood near the door to the Pump Room and cast a look around the room. There she was. Mr. Doherty had stopped Belle and Mr. Baily, but Baily was not giving up his position at Belle's side. What man would?

Fritz shook his head. A fool. An absolute fool. That is who would give up a prize such as Belle.

"Ah, Mr. Norman," Mr. Wesley said, "you are not leaving without taking a turn of the room with my Charlotte, are you?"

"I am afraid I am."

"Oh, that is a shame."

"Indeed, it is," Fritz agreed for the sake of the lady holding her grandfather's arm. "But I have a call to make."

"Do you?" Curiosity was clearly written across Mr. Wesley's face.

Fritz nodded.

Mr. Wesley glanced at his granddaughter and then whispered, "Another lady?"

"A friend and his wife." His answer caused the man in front of him to visibly relax.

"Neither he nor his wife are ill, are they?"

Fritz's eyes once again fell on the prettiest lady in the room. "No, no," he assured Mr. Wesley. "They are both well. I am just calling for the pleasure of calling." And to collect on a favour owed him by both his friend and that friend's wife.

There were many things which Fritz was not, but at the top of the list was the fact that he, Fredrick Norman, was not a fool. No, he assured himself with one final look in Belle's direction, he was most definitely not a fool.

Chapter 10

"My dear, you are looking utterly fatigued."

Belle wrapped her arm around her aunt's as they made their way toward home. "I am, Aunt Augusta. I truly am. Would you be terribly put out if we stayed at home tonight?"

To be perfectly honest, she had had her fill of society. Not because the people she met with were overly disagreeable, it was the need to smile and be charming which was beginning to grate and take a toll.

"I am not opposed to a quiet evening at home." Her aunt paused. "Are you certain you only require rest? You are not becoming ill, are you?"

"I am well," Belle assured her aunt. "I am just tired."

For a distance, they walked on in what Belle considered to be welcome silence. Her weary ears and mind welcomed the peace that quietness brought. However, she new the peace would be fleeting, as, soon, thoughts of Fritz would once again enter her mind. It did not matter that she had resolved to give him up, he still occupied a large portion of her thoughts and filled her heart to overflowing with an ache which nothing could ever remove. She swallowed and blinked rapidly against the tears which threatened.

"I heard Miss Philip questioning her niece about Mr. Norman."

"Please," Belle begged, "speak of anything but him."

"I think you will find this of interest."

"I do not think my tired mind can find anything to be of interest at the moment." She brushed at a wayward tear.

Her aunt was silent but only for a moment. "It seems Miss James has decided that she and Mr. Norman will not suit as anything more than friends."

"Oh?"

"And it seems he is not unduly disturbed by such a thing. In fact, Miss James said that he seemed relieved."

"Oh?" It was the only word which Belle's mind and lips seemed capable of forming.

"Her aunt was truly disappointed by this turn of events, as was her mother, and I can understand why. Mr. Norman is as fine a gentleman as I would wish to have anyone I loved marry." With her free hand, Aunt Augusta squeezed Belle's forearm where it wrapped around her own arm.

It was a small gesture, but the meaning and comfort which lay behind it and her aunt's words were not insignificant. Belle knew just how dearly her aunt loved her.

"Miss James said," her aunt continued, leaning a bit closer to Belle and using a softer voice, "that he admitted to having lost his heart long ago and not having one to give to anyone."

"Oh, Aunt."

Another tear slid down her cheek and was quickly brushed away. To think that the sorrow which her family had caused him still kept him from finding happiness was nearly too much to bear. She would gladly disown each and every one of them and sail away to the furthest reaches of the earth if it could bring him happiness.

"He loves you," her aunt whispered. "He still loves you."

"But it can never be," Belle protested as they turned down the street which would lead them to her aunt's home.

"Why? Because my brother is an idiot?"

"Yes."

"What can he do? Start rumors that Mr. Norman is not a capable physician?"

"Aunt, I am tired." And she was quite certain that if they were to speak about him much longer, she would cause quite a scene by dissolving into a sobbing mass right here in the street.

"Very well, I shall not press you on this point now, but it needs to be considered, my darling niece. Mr. Norman is well-established with many who adore him and credit him with outstanding care. Your father's words would mean little."

The remainder of their walk home was blessedly free from conversation, though it was by no means silent as Belle attempted to ignore her aunt's words while her heart pushed them hopefully forward.

"Annabelle," her aunt called to her before Belle could ascend more than two steps of the staircase which would take her to her room. "My home is not so large as some, but I am certain it has ample room for three people to live in it."

Belle's brow furrowed.

Aunt Augusta came to the bottom of the staircase. "I am saying that you will always have a home no matter your decision regarding Mr. Norman." Her lips tipped up. "I dare say we could even fit a few children into one of the rooms." She turned away from Belle. "Have a good rest, my darling. I will be stitching or reading if you should need me."

Belle stared after her aunt. *Have a good rest? Have a good rest?* Of all the ridiculous things to say after bringing up things which she knew very well Belle would not be able to push aside.

She huffed in exasperation and took the stairs to her room quickly. She would wash her face and change her dress, and then, she would take a book to the garden and sit in the bit of sun that darted in and out of the clouds.

She removed her bonnet as she pushed the door to her room open. Tossing it on the bed, she began the work of unfastening her coat while she crossed to her dressing table. A glance in the mirror told her that her hair would need a bit of attention but not much. She pushed her coat off her shoulders as her gaze fell on a missive sitting on the dressing table. Quickly, she finished removing her coat and broke open the letter and darted a look at the signature. *Mrs. Grace Blakesley.*

My dear friend,

Belle smiled at the appellation, but her smile faltered and fell as she read the rest of the short note. She sat down heavily on the chair in front of her mirror and poked a few wayward hairs back into place, smoothed the top of her coiffure with a brush, and then, after a quick splash of water on her face and taking care of any other refreshing that needed to be seen to, Belle snatched up her hat and coat and flew down the stairs to find her aunt.

"I thought you were going to rest?" her aunt questioned in surprise when Belle rushed into the room, her coat half on and half off.

"I need to see a friend."

Her aunt was on her feet and ringing for a maid. "Whatever is the matter?"

"This." Belle handed Grace's letter to Aunt Augusta.

"Have the carriage readied as quickly as can be

managed," Aunt Augusta said to the maid who entered. "Oh, this is not good. The poor girl."

~*~*~

An interminably long half-hour later, Belle and her aunt were being led up the stairs to the drawing room at the Blakesley's house.

"Is she well?" Belle placed a hand on Fritz's arm as he exited the drawing room before they entered.

"She is, but I am going to send for something should she need it for sleep."

"And Mr. Blakesley?"

"He is distraught because his wife is distraught, of course, but he will take good care of her." He gave a small bow and hurried down the stairs.

Belle crossed the room and took the place at Grace's side that Mr. Blakesley had vacated at Belle and her aunt's entrance.

"I will give you time to talk," he said to Belle before crouching down in front of his wife and whispering to Grace that he would return soon and if she needed anything, she was just to send word.

Grace attempted a small smile for him, but it was weak at best. Belle had never seen Grace without a smile at the ready, but, while it was a trifle shocking, it was understandable.

"How are you?" Belle took Grace's hand and squeezed it. "We came as quickly as we could."

Grace pulled in a deep breath and released it. "I am better now than I was when I wrote that note. My husband is such a dear, you know."

"I do."

"And then, Mr. Norman arrived even before Walter could send for him, and he has been a great blessing. He assures me that the shock of the news I received will lift eventually, and he seemed excessively pleased that I had sent for you. He kept saying that you would be just the person to sit with me for a time."

"I suppose it is because I have lost a brother," Belle said, but Grace shook her head.

"It is not that. My sister still lives. He said you were the gentlest, most compassionate lady he knew and that your very presence would be enough to bring me peace." Her lips quivered. "He thinks very highly of you."

Belle rested a hand on her rapidly beating heart. To hear herself spoken of so fondly by the man who should hate her because of her family was unsettling in the extreme. However, now was not the time to think of herself.

"He is a dear man, is he not?" she replied with a smile. "Now, how can I be of service?"

Grace's head tipped and her brow furrowed. "Are you not going to ask me about what happened?"

Belle shook her head. "You will tell me when you can." She offered her friend an extra handkerchief she had brought just for that purpose.

"It is no wonder he adores you." Grace dabbed at her eyes. "I wish you would consider him."

"How can I?" Belle replied. "After what my father has done to him?" She shook her head. "How could I ask him to be tied to the man who did him harm?" She blew out a breath. "I refused him, and for such a foolish reason."

"You refused him?" Aunt Augusta said in surprise.

Belle nodded. No one, except her mother, knew about that refusal. "He wished to run away to Scotland, but I did not feel I could leave my mother since I knew Father would never allow me to see her again if I did such a thing. I would be utterly cut off – no funds, no family."

"That does not seem a foolish reason to refuse an elopement," Grace said.

"I should not be talking about this now. I am here to help you."

"I do not mind," Grace said. "In fact, it is nice to be able to think of something other than Felicity right now – even if the story is not a happy one."

"Are you certain?"

Grace nodded.

"Very well. I will continue. My mother and I had always been close when I was growing up. She was the one I ran to when Father was being impossible – which was often. Mother would dry my tears and assure me that she would speak to him. That was all the reassurance I needed when I was young. A hug and a kind word, and I believed her. Nothing ever changed with Father, but I felt heard."

She should have realized that her mother was only saying what was necessary to quell a distraught child, but why would a child doubt her dearly loved parent?

"And she was not speaking to your father," Aunt Augusta surmised.

"No, she was not. Or she was not unless it was something which she thought would please him."

She shook her head at her foolishness. "Even if it was a secret she was not meant to share."

Grace gasped.

"Mr. Norman?" Aunt Augusta asked softly.

Belle nodded. "I always wondered how my father or brother discovered us every time we attempted to sneak away for a walk. My father can only think of himself, and because of that, my mother has suffered neglect on occasion. I know this. Anyone privy to our family's affairs knows this. It is how he is with everyone. No one comes ahead of himself. Ever. My mother, as I suppose is natural to a point, longed for her husband's approval. She used my confidences to earn his favour, and it seems to have worked. Father has been far more attentive to her since she saved him from a disagreeable connection."

"How did you discover this?" Aunt Augusta asked.

Belle closed her eyes and attempted not to relive the scene in her mind as she spoke. "Mother wept when I told her I was considering marrying without Father's approval. I told her how much I loved Fritz and just how devastated I would be to live without him. But her tears over never seeing me again, swayed me to wait. She promised to speak to Father. And she did, for that was why Father and Andrew decided they must do something to destroy Fritz. I know this because Father told me, as he was laughing over my desolation when Fritz left." Her father was an ugly, ugly man, and her mother was just as horrible if not worse. "My mother lost me that day. I have never been able to be more than civil to her since."

"Oh, how dreadful," Grace said. "Family members can be so dreadful."

"They can be," Aunt August agreed. "They most certainly can be. Oh, my poor dear girls, what both of you have suffered."

"My plight is not so grave as Belle's," Grace protested. "My sister's life is in shambles, and we fear she might once again attempt to take it, but I am loved by my parents. Neither of them would do anything to harm me." She squeezed Belle's hand. "I cannot be the mother you should have had, but I can be a friend who keeps your confidences and stands by your side."

Belle shook her head and dried her eyes. "I am here to help you, and, instead, you are extending yourself to me. Mr. Norman is wrong. You, Mrs.

Blakesley, are the most compassionate lady anyone could ever meet."

"No, he is not wrong," Aunt Augusta inserted, "I think the two of you are more alike than unlike in this." She shrugged and dabbed her eyes when both Belle and Grace looked at her. "Mr. Norman is not just the finest physician in all of Bath. He is one of the noblest men I have ever met, and from what I have observed and especially from what I know of Mr. Blakesley and his wife, Mr. Norman surrounds himself with people of the very best character. One does very well to be counted amongst his friends."

Chapter 11

Walter placed a glass of cider in front of Fritz, and then took a seat in front of his desk. Fritz looked up from the missive he was writing and gave a nod of appreciation, but he did not take a sip of the beverage until he had sealed his note and sent it on its way to his assistant.

"Thank you for the use of your study." He picked up the glass from the desk and took a gulp before sitting down in the chair next to Walter rather than the one behind the desk in which he had been sitting. "I will have everything I need for your wife within the half-hour, though I doubt she will need much more than you..." His voice trailed off as he watched the liquid in his glass follow the swirling motion of his hand. "And Belle," he added, lifting the glass to his lips.

"Your description of Miss Chapman to my wife

was rather impressive for a man who claims he can remove the lady from his heart and replace her with someone else."

Fritz could only nod his agreement with his friend's direct and pointed statement. "I was wrong. She cannot be replaced."

"What about Miss James? I thought you told Grace that Miss James might make an excellent wife."

"And she will. However, she will not be my wife." He emptied his glass of the remaining cider. "She agrees. We parted amicably."

"You what?" Walter placed his empty glass next to Fritz's on the desk before them.

"We came to an understanding that we do not suit."

"And when did this happen?"

"Today, at the Pump Room. I could not pay attention to a thing she was saying because all I could see was Belle on the arm of that blasted Mr. Baily." He blew out a breath. "My inattention did not go unnoticed, and when brought to my attention, it was followed by a request that we remain friends and naught else." His lips tipped up in a half-smile. "I have not been so relieved since

Mrs. Hall's youngest opened her eyes and asked for a drink after two days of fitful fever."

Walter chuckled. "It is a very good thing then that you have parted from Miss James if being with her reminds you of watching over a gravely ill child."

"Indeed," Fritz said with a chuckle of his own. He had not realized just how much he had dreaded the thought of marrying someone other than Belle until he had felt that wave of relief wash over him. To be sure, he had never found the idea to be appealing. It had just seemed necessary. However, it was not. He could not find another to take Belle's place. He simply could not. Dealing with a perpetually broken heart was better than entering halfheartedly into a marriage.

"It was indeed a moment of clarity," he continued.

"And what is your plan from here?"

He glanced at his friend. Walter was smiling as if he already knew the answer to that question. "I believe I must speak with Miss Chapman and see if all hope is truly lost or not."

Walter's smile faded, and his eyes grew serious. "And if all hope is lost?"

That was the question, was it not? Fritz had no idea how he would survive such a thing. He shook his head. "Truthfully, I do not know, but I would imagine I would begin by cancelling all my appointments for a week and attempting to pickle myself in a few bottles of your best cider."

Walter chuckled and clapped Fritz on the shoulder. "I will supply you with enough cider to preserve you, but not enough to be your demise. However, I do hope it does not come to that."

"Likewise," Fritz agreed. "Likewise," he repeated.

"I very much doubt it will," Walter assured him as he rose from his seat. "As I have said from the moment when I met your Belle, I think your fears are for naught." He poured two fingers worth of cider into Fritz's glass and then his own. "Now, how may I assist you? You did a fabulous job of helping me secure my wife. Therefore, it is only appropriate that I attempt to return the favour."

"I had hoped that your wife might help me arrange a time to meet with Belle by chance in the gardens, but that will not do now."

"A stroll in the sunshine would not do Grace

any harm." Walter tipped his glass and studied it with a pensive look on his face.

"I would not suggest it for a day or two," Fritz said softly. "A pretty aspect and an open window will have to make do for the present. Having to appear cheerful in front of others when a person is grieving or recovering from a shock is not helpful."

He shrugged. "That is why I would need a week with some cider. I required a fortnight of indulging in self-pity before I was able to even contemplate where I would seek to begin again when Belle and I parted those many years ago."

"But your sorrow was of a different and deeper sort than my wife's is," Walter protested. "However, Grace's heart is tender." His jaw clenched as he shook his head. "How can a gentleman do what Ramsey did? If I knew where to find him, I would see him suffer for causing my wife pain."

Fritz's eyebrows rose. "Is it not her sister, who was prevented from throwing herself into the sea from a cliff, which is the issue."

"No. It is the selfishness of Ramsey." Walter turned in his seat to face his friend. "I will admit to not particularly liking Felicity. She, herself, has been a selfish and thoughtless creature." He once again shook his head. "However, she was persuaded – perhaps it did not take a great deal of persuasion, I do not know about that – but she was led to believe the man would marry her. He had all but made the offer. He had even scheduled a time to present his offer. Yet, he runs off into the night with another lady when he knows full well that he has left Felicity ruined and quite possibly with his child. *That*. That is the catalyst of all the present calamity."

"You do not fault Miss Love?" Fritz found that hard to believe.

"No, I fault her for being stupid, but I can understand her desperation, I suppose. You know the sorts of whispers which will follow her as an unwed lady who is with child, and if she truly loved him..."

Fritz nodded. "Then, the bleakness of her future grows because of the devastation of her heart."

"Precisely, and that is why I should very much like to make the man suffer. A good thrashing is nothing compared to the pain of the heart."

"No truer words have been spoken." Fritz knew exactly how fragile a heart could be and just how impossible it was to help it heal from some wounds.

"Not even Felicity deserves such agony." Walter blew out a breath. "Especially because her sorrow will not be hers alone." His fingers drummed a rapid beat on his leg.

Fritz could not help but smile at how greatly Walter was devoted to and in love with Mrs. Blakesley. He would hate to be the person to bear the full force of Walter's displeasure for causing his wife any unease. As it was, Mr. Ramsey was a fortunate fellow to be absent from Bath and in an unknown location. Hopefully, the man would stay hidden for some time as Fritz knew that Walter's anger would dissipate with his wife's recovery, and, while the scoundrel deserved whatever Walter gave him, Fritz did not wish to see his friend's name or that of his wife attached to any whispers of scandal. That would only make the situation more grievous for Mrs. Blakesley and by extension, Walter.

"We should likely go see that your Mrs. Blakesley is well," Fritz suggested just as the door to the study opened and a parcel, containing the required teas and tinctures, arrived for him.

He rummaged through the box and withdrew a bag. "A bit of tea might be the perfect way to begin."

He handed the bag to Walter. "Lavender and chamomile. For the nerves – and several other ailments – but today it is for the nerves. Then, after we have had tea, we will leave you to comfort your wife as you see fit. There are directions for each of these."

He placed a folded page on top of the contents in the box and, leaving it on Walter's desk, crossed to the door. However, Walter blocked his exit.

"Stay here."

Fritz's brow furrowed. "I would like to see my patient to assess her condition."

Walter shook his head. "Not yet. Allow me to see her first. Allow me five minutes."

"I do not see why. It is not as if Mrs. Blakesley is alone and two more entering the room will overwhelm her."

Walter's lips curled into a smile. "No, she is not alone, and neither should you be." He turned and hurried from the room calling a "five minutes, just five minutes" over his shoulder.

Of all the strange things! Perhaps Fritz should

note on that set of instructions that Walter partake of all the tinctures with his wife, for the man seemed to be acting very oddly. He pulled out his pocket watch and made note of the time as he paced the room.

Back and forth. Back and forth. Over and over for what seemed like five minutes.

He checked his watch a second time. Two minutes! He huffed. Time certainly crept along slowly when confined.

Again, he crossed the room. As he was turning to walk back to the door, it opened.

"Fritz!" Belle's hand flew to her heart. Her gaze shifted from him to the desk. "Mr. Blakesley told his wife you had brought a box of remedies."

He nodded and motioned to the desk without removing his eyes from her. He should say something now, but all he seemed capable of doing was studying how beautiful she was — the curve of her neck, the deep blue of her eyes, the waves of her hair that no amount of combing could remove, the rosy hue of her lips. She was, to him, beauty personified.

"Grace was curious to see them, and Mr. Blakesley asked me if I would mind fetching them."

She crossed to the desk and picked up the box. "I was, of course, more than willing to oblige."

She took one step toward the door but hesitated. "I thought you had left. Why are you here in the study?" She placed the box she held back on the desk. "I can leave so that you can attend Mrs. Blakesley." Her eyes were fixed on the box, and her words were only just above a whisper.

"Please, do not leave." He took the few steps necessary to stand next to her. Bless his friend for allowing him this opportunity – no matter if it resulted in a shattered heart or a joyous one. "Please, Belle. Please, stay."

She looked up at him. Tears clung to the rims of her eyes. How he longed to take her in his arms and tell her everything was going to be put to right. However, he could not. That privilege had not been given to him.

"I am so sorry, Fritz. My father and brother..." A tear escaped her eye and slid down her cheek.

"Shhh," he whispered as his hand cupped her cheek and his thumb brushed that tear away. "It was not your doing."

"I should have gone with you. I wish I had." She

was trembling, and he could not resist holding her any longer.

He pulled her into his embrace and exhaled deeply. She did not resist but allowed her soft form to be firmly wrapped inside his arms. How wonderful it felt to hold her.

"Would you go now?" He asked quietly. "If I asked you to run away with me now, would you?"

Her head shook against his jacket, and his heart sank.

"How could I ask you to be tied to my father?"

He held her firmly against him, fearing that at any moment she would disappear.

"I do not care about that now any more than I cared then." His hold on her relaxed. As much as he wished to pursue her with no thought for anything but his own happiness, he could not. "I cannot ask you," he said sadly. "Oh, Belle, I wish I could, but I cannot. However, you must know that it is not because of your father."

"He would still try to ruin you just as he did then. I know he would." She pulled back and looked into his eyes.

"He cannot do that, for he already has."

Her brow furrowed. "But you are successful.

You are not ruined. I know that your practice is not where you would wish it to be, but you have triumphed over his scheming."

He shook his head. "It is not that. While I am well-established in my profession and have neither want of house nor food, I am yet missing the one thing which I need – the only thing I need."

The furrow had not left her brow, and her eyes shifted between his as if searching for an answer. "What is that?"

"You."

A small, tentative smile crept across her lips. "You do not hate me?"

"Hate you? How could I ever hate you? I love you, Belle. I shall always love you."

She rested her cheek against his chest. "And I love you, so why can you not ask me to run away with you?"

"How could I separate you from your mother?"

She laughed a small bitter laugh. "My father has already done that."

When he pulled back and looked down at her in confusion, she related to him all the treachery in which her mother had played a part.

"Ah, Belle," he said as he rubbed her back. "It

grieves me more deeply than you can possibly know to hear that you have suffered so."

How could a parent treat a daughter in such a fashion? It was not natural. The thought caused him to scowl until the realization dawned on him that his reason for not pursuing Belle no longer existed. Then, a smile tipped his lips as his heart fluttered with hopeful excitement. It may be that her father might still try to ruin him, but would he if it would bring disgrace to him through his daughter if she was already Mrs. Norman before her father even discovered they had found one another again?

"Marry me."

She looked at him with wide eyes. "Do you mean it? You would marry me after all my family has done to you?"

"Yes, and despite anything they might yet try to do. Please, Belle, will you marry me?"

She nodded as tears once again gathered in her eyes and a smile suffused her features. "If you will have me, I am yours."

Had happier words ever been spoken? Fritz thought not, and when he lowered his head to claim her lips in a kiss that was equal parts passion and reverence, he knew it to be true. There was no greater happiness than this.

Chapter 12

He loved her. Tears slid down Belle's cheeks as she tangled her fingers in Fritz's hair, holding him to her as if she needed his kisses to sustain her. *He loved her.* There was no more wonderful thought in all the world. How often had she longed for him to say that to her once again? Nearly every day for six years. How often had she cried because she had thought she would never hear him say that to her ever again? Just as often as she had wished to hear it.

He pulled back, breaking their kiss so that he could brush her tears away. "Do not cry," he whispered.

"It cannot be helped. The joy I feel..." She shook her head for she did not know how to accurately describe it. "It is overwhelming." Delightfully, wonderfully overwhelming. It seemed to fill every place in her. "I love you."

He smiled and rested his forehead against hers. "And I love you." His arms pulled her more firmly against him. "We should marry quickly. I do not wish to leave time for something to separate us. I am not certain my heart would survive losing you again."

"Oh, Fritz! I am so sorry." How foolish she had been!

"Please, Belle, it was not your doing. Do not think that it was."

"But I refused you."

He shook his head. "Not because you wished to. I knew it then, and I know it now."

"But the pain it caused you is so great."

"Was it greater than yours?" His eyes searched hers as she considered his question.

"No," she finally admitted. "Or, at least, I do not think so. But then, who can tell who bears more sorrow?"

He kissed her gently. "Precisely my point, my dear." He sighed contentedly. "You are mine. Finally, you are mine – or you will be." He straightened and loosened his hold on her. "And that brings me back to the fact that we should marry quickly. No banns. Just a common license and a parson, unless you would like to leave for Gretna Green right now."

The fact that he was as eager as she to be married was comforting and rather thrilling. "What about your patients? It is not as if a trip to Scotland and back can be made before tomorrow."

"I have an assistant. He can see to whatever needs doing until we return."

She played with his earlobe while she thought about it. Dashing away to Scotland with him was still as exhilarating a prospect as it had been six years ago.

"What thought is causing that scowl?"

"Was I scowling?" She had not thought she was.

"You were."

"I was merely thinking about my aunt and the Blakesleys." She shook her head. She should not be thinking about anything but him. "I hesitated to run away with you before. I will not do it again. If you wish me to, I will go home and gather what I need right now, and we can be off."

His replying grin was beautiful. How she had missed seeing that smile.

"I think we should likely tell them of our plans," he countered. "I honestly do not think even your aunt would attempt to prevent our departure, and I think that our happy news would be most beneficial to Mrs. Blakesley."

"Oh! Grace! I had forgotten I was supposed to take that box of remedies up to her."

Fritz laughed. "I doubt she expects them immediately, for I imagine her husband told her that he had left me here on purpose."

She blinked. "What do you mean he left you here?"

"I was on my way to check on Mrs. Blakesley when Walter prevented me from leaving the study and told me to wait five minutes before returning to the drawing room. He gave no real explanation as to why, but I obliged."

The whole scheme began to come into view in such a beautiful way that, once again, Belle felt tears threatening. "You were waiting for me." What a wonderful thought!

Fritz nodded. "Though I did not know it."

"How did he know you and I would welcome sceing each other?"

Fritz released her from his embrace so that he

could cup her face while kissing her. "I had told him that my plan was to speak to you at some point and discover if all hope was lost or not. I realized just today, at the Pump Room, that I could never love anyone but you. No matter how I might try to find another, there is only one lady who will ever claim my heart."

"And so, Mr. Blakesley arranged for us to have an opportunity to speak." Her heart wanted to laugh with delight at Mr. Blakesley's scheming.

"He is a good friend, is he not?"

She could not disagree with that. "The best. He is absolutely the best friend anyone could ever have." She shook her head in bewilderment. "How different things are! To think that there are people scheming to see us together rather than to tear us apart."

She moved to the desk and picked up the box of remedies. "You are right. We should tell them, and if any of them should wish for us to marry here so that they can be present, I think we should honor that."

She moved toward the door, pausing on her way to kiss him once again. "You know, my aunt knew of our past before she ever took you on as her physician, and I suspect that is why she was so insistent that my father send me to her."

"She does like to play at matchmaking," Fritz agreed as he followed behind her. "She was forever suggesting ladies to both me and Walter." He stopped two steps below her on the stairs. "When was it agreed that you were to come to her?"

Belle remembered the conversation well. Her father had called her into his study, where her mother was already seated, and told her of his disappointment in her inability to find an acceptable husband. His disgust at the thought of her wasting her looks and not adding to the family's standing was palpable in every word that proceeded from his mouth. Her mother had not even shed a tear, but she had rather looked pleased by the situation.

"It was September when I was told I would be given until January to find a husband, or I would be relegated to the station of a companion and a spinster. Why? What are you thinking?"

Fritz shook his head and smiled. "I believe that is very close to the time when your aunt stopped suggesting ladies to me. I had thought she grew tired of my constant refusals, but it seems she had merely changed tack."

Belle waited for him at the top of the stairs. "I am glad she did. I should have been very sorry to arrive in Bath and find you married. I must admit that I had hoped over the years that you had found some sort of happiness but only because I wished to think of you as no longer injured, though such thoughts never truly brought me the solace for which I wished."

"I had assumed you would be married by now. How could you not be when you are so beautiful? You must know that I did not wish for it. I just knew it must be, and I had resigned myself to having lost you forever."

"Yes, yes," she agreed with some force. "I, too, had resigned myself to someone else being your wife until I saw you at that ball and discovered you were not married. Then, the small hope that you still loved me, which I had held in my heart all those years, tried to push its way forward, but I knew it could not be."

He nodded as if he knew exactly what she spoke.

"I thought from how you avoided me that you must hate me but were too polite to act on it."

His hand was on the door handle. "I avoided you because every time I saw you I wanted to take you in my arms and persuade you to give me another chance, but I could not bear the thought of being the cause of a breach between you and your mother. I knew how much she meant to you. However, it seems we were both wrong in our assumptions."

"Delightfully wrong," she agreed, and she had never been so glad to be wrong in all her life. "What are you doing?" she asked when he took the box that she held from her and placed it on the floor.

"Freeing your hands," he explained before he opened the door just enough to slide the box in with his foot. "There." He pulled the door firmly closed and while one hand held the handle to prevent someone from opening the door, his other arm drew her close. "We have six years for which to atone."

Those were the last words he spoke to her for several minutes until the door beside them finally opened when Fritz forgot himself and moved to embrace her completely.

"I see all hope is not lost."

"Blakesley," Fritz growled, "go away." There was a squeal of delight from within the room before the door closed and Fritz once again kissed her. Then, with a sigh and much sooner than she wished, he released her from his embrace. "I think they know our happy news."

"It does seem so." Nervously, she straightened her clothing and touched her hair.

"You look perfect," Fritz whispered.

"But do I look as if I have been kissing you?"

He nodded. "That is what makes you look so perfectly perfect, and it does not matter anyway as they likely all saw us kissing as it is."

"But it is one thing to be caught kissing and another to look as if one has been kissed."

An eyebrow arched. "I think they are the same."

She was not so certain of that. It would be much harder for those she was about to face to forget what they had seen if her appearance bore evidence of the impropriety.

"We are to marry. All will be well," he whispered as he opened the door and led her into the sitting room.

Grace was beaming and dabbing her eyes with a handkerchief while her husband sat next to her looking as pleased as punch, and Aunt Augusta left her seat and crossed the room to give Belle a hug as soon as the pair had stepped into the room.

It was not at all what Belle expected. Her aunt was not the sort to be so openly demonstrative with her affection. A small smile, a knowing look, a pat of the hand, a squeeze of an arm – those were all ways Aunt Augusta displayed her affection. An embrace was reserved for when they were in private and Belle was feeling sad. Even then, it was not the engulfing hug that she was currently giving Belle.

"Oh, I am so happy." She pulled back and looked at Belle. "I had hoped. I had hoped so dearly." Then, she hugged Belle again before turning her attention to Fritz. "May I?" she asked.

Fritz looked from Aunt Augusta to Belle and back. "I... I suppose."

He had barely gotten the words out before Aunt Augusta was giving him a quick embrace.

"Do not worry," she assured him. "I will not do that often. I never do. But I am just so delighted." She clapped her hands. "Do you need a new dress?"

"Aunt!"

"Every bride needs a new dress," her aunt protested. "And I assume from what you were doing in the corridor that you are getting married." One eyebrow arched as she attempted to affect a stern look. Her success, however, was limited. Very limited.

"Perhaps when we return from Scotland." Belle bit back a smile at how wide her aunt's eyes grew.

"Scotland!" Grace cried. "Are you marrying in Scotland?" There was a decided note of excitement in Grace's voice.

"We do not wish to wait," Belle replied. "My father has prevented us once before."

"The dress we ordered will have to suffice," was all her aunt said before she turned and retook her seat. "It will be ready the day after tomorrow. Can you wait that long?"

"You do not mind if we do not marry here?"

Aunt Augusta shrugged. "I think the time between now and when you are wed would be the same if you got a common license here as it would be if you travelled to Scotland, but I can appreciate your desire to be where your father is not." She ran a hand over her lap to smooth a skirt that held not a wrinkle. "I shall even be content to see Mr. Spencer while you are gone." Again, an eyebrow arched. However, this time it was paired with a much more effective stern expression. "So long as you are not gone too long. Two weeks. I think I can manage for two weeks." Her lips pursed. "Perhaps three if I must."

"I am so very happy for you," Grace said. "It is the perfect remedy for my hurting heart."

"Well," Aunt Augusta said with a smile. "Mr. Norman is the best physician in Bath."

"That he is," Walter agreed loudly.

Beside her, Fritz laughed. "I cannot and will not take credit for this remedy, for I believe, Mrs. Blakesley, that it was your husband's doing."

Grace smiled affectionately at Mr. Blakesley. "He is very clever, is he not?"

"Yes," Fritz said, lifting Belle's hand to his lips and giving it a kiss, "happily so. Very happily so."

Chapter 13

A week later, music was once again swirling around Fritz as he tripped his way lightly through the steps of a dance in the Upper Rooms. However, this time, he was not searching for a replacement for the lady he loved. This time, he had a marriage license just waiting to be used when their appointment with the parson finally arrived.

Two more days were all that was needed. In two days from today and less than ten from when he had secured Belle's agreement to marry him, he would have the lady he loved at his side as his wife for the remainder of his life. Six years of separation and the pain which had accompanied them dimmed in comparison to the happiness that lay before him.

"I cannot put my finger on it," Miss James said as her hand joined Fritz's, "but you seem not just happier tonight than you were the last time we spoke but something more."

"I am," Fritz said before they were parted. He was much more than just happy.

"At peace," Miss James said when they next met several steps and turns later. "That is what it is. You are not just happier. You seem to be at peace."

"I am. I very much am." He had never felt more contented than he presently did.

"Is it Miss Chapman?" Miss James asked softly. "Is she the one of whom you were thinking when you told me you did not have a heart to give?"

Fritz turned away from her as he followed the dance pattern. He and Belle had kept their meetings confined to either her aunt's house or the Blakesley's home. They had only once in the last week ventured as far as meeting in Sydney Gardens for a walk, and even that had been staged as the chance meeting of one happening upon the other. They had taken every precaution they could to not let anyone know of their attachment until tonight.

Tonight, Mrs. Blakesley was making her first appearance at a soiree since receiving the news of her sister being with child and having attempted to take her life. Neither Fritz nor Belle wanted to be anywhere else tonight but here, helping their friend through what could be a challenging evening.

For Mrs. Blakesley's sake, they were willing to share their joyous secret with those gathered here. Not that they were telling anyone that they were getting married. No, that fact would remain an absolute secret to all except those whom they trusted most in their acquaintance. However, everyone else would most certainly know after tonight that Belle was the lady he had selected to court.

"Is she? Is the lady Miss Chapman?" Miss James asked again when taking his arm at the conclusion of the dance.

Fritz smiled. "She is."

Miss James sighed. "How wonderful to find the one you thought you had lost. You had thought you had lost her, had you not?" she added quickly. "It seemed as if you did when we were speaking that day."

"You are not incorrect. I truly thought her lost to me forever, but Providence has smiled down on me and given me a second chance for which I will be eternally grateful."

"She is beautiful, and from all I have heard, it is not just her face which bears her beauty."

"You are correct. It is her heart that makes the beauty of her face and the elegance of her figure pale as if they were no more becoming than a common portrait completed by a painter of no renown."

Again, Miss James sighed. It was a wistful sound. "With any luck, I shall find someone to think of me that way one day."

"You will," Fritz assured her. "You have a good heart and a pretty face, and," he leaned a trifle closer to her and lowered his voice, "your aunt is not easily put off. How could you fail with all those things working in your favour?"

Miss James laughed. "Thank you, Mr. Norman. I pray you are correct."

"I am certain I am. Thank you, Miss James, for the pleasure of a dance with a friend," he said when they had come to where her aunt and mother waited.

"Mr. Norman, you do us such a great honor by dancing with Margaret after... well... your last conversation," Miss Philips looked around before adding softly, "in the Pump Room."

"It was an amicable parting," he reassured Miss Philips. "We remain friends."

The lady before him once again glanced around like a nervous mouse intent upon getting a piece of cheese but not knowing if the cat was watching. "I had thought so, but then, when I got your message that you would not be able to see me the day after tomorrow, I began to fret."

"I did not assign your call to Mr. Spenser because I did not wish to see you. I am otherwise engaged on that day." And his wedding was not an appointment he would put off for anyone. Mr. Spenser was a capable surgeon who had gained a great deal of knowledge about many things during his time working with Fritz.

Miss Philips smiled. "That is very comforting to hear. I should hate to have to find another physician, for I am not certain I could find one who was your equal."

"I assure you that you will have no need of finding another physician for so long as I am in Bath and practising."

His companion's shoulders dropped comfortably as she sighed.

"That is what I told you, Aunt."

"Yes, yes, you did, but I could not be at ease until I heard it from Mr. Norman. Your thoughts were just as much speculation as mine were."

Miss James did not look convinced by that, but she turned from her aunt back to Fritz. "We do not wish to keep you from your next dance partner."

"Do you have one? Is it Miss Wesley?" Miss Philips asked.

"I do have another partner engaged for this next set of dances, but it is not Miss Wesley. It is Miss Chapman."

"A second dance?"

Fritz was certain he had never seen Miss Philips's eyes grow so large in surprise in all the time he had known her.

"Yes, a second dance, and if she were to allow me, I would seek a third."

"Three sets?" Miss Philips's hand lay on top of her heart. "Three sets?" she repeated.

"Yes, if she would allow me, but I doubt she will."

"But three sets? People would think..."

"I know what they would think, and they would not be wrong."

"Indeed?" There was an excited glint in the lady's eyes.

Fritz nodded. "Your niece's notions about marriage, of which we spoke the last time we met, are not strange and, happily, very happily, they are entirely possible for some." Then, before the delight in her expression could be turned into a litany of words, he took his leave of Miss Philips, her sister, and her niece and hurried on his way to find Belle.

"Mr. Norman," Miss Wesley attached herself to his arm, "allow me to walk with you to wherever you are going. Please." There was a note of desperation in her tone.

"Where is your grandfather?"

"Detained in speaking to a friend. I was just strolling the perimeter of the room."

"By yourself?"

"Yes, I know I likely should not have been, but I did not think it would be an issue." She glanced anxiously over her shoulder. "But *he* is here," she whispered.

"He?"

"Do you not remember the popinjay about whom my grandfather told you?"

"Do you mean the gentleman who is more fascinated with his looks and status than anything else?"

She nodded. "The very one."

"And he is here?"

"Yes, is it not the most dreadful thing ever?"

"I suppose it must be."

"Oh, it is. I assure you that it is. I am not a flighty female, Mr. Norman. I am very sensible." Her brow furrowed and a pained expression settled on her delicate features. "He is not. He is the vainest gentleman in all the world, and he thinks that since he likes me, I must like him in return."

"And do you like him?"

She sighed. "I am sensible. I have always been sensible."

"I am sure you have been. It is what your grandfather has told me."

"Liking him would not be sensible."

"You have not answered the question, Miss Wesley. Do you like him?"

She scowled and glanced over her shoulder again. "Despite all that is sensible, yes, but it cannot be. I cannot like a gentleman who is so self appreciative! I simply cannot."

"I am afraid there is only one remedy," Fritz said as they drew near where Belle was waiting for him.

"What is it?" Miss Wesley asked eagerly.

"You must find another to take his place, or you must, at least, attempt to find someone to take his place. If you can find another, you will prove yourself correct that you simply cannot love such a person as this nonsensical gentleman. However, if you cannot find another, then you will have to accept that sometimes even the most sensible person is wrong."

Miss Wesley sighed. "That seems logical, but are you certain there is not a simpler way? Is there not, perhaps, a set of exercises, for instance, that I might do daily to rid me of this desire to see him?"

Fritz chuckled. "No. There is no other way. You must decipher what your heart says. Is it a passing fancy or something more enduring?" He looked at Belle and then back to Miss Wesley. "Miss Wesley, have you met Miss Chapman?"

Miss Wesley's eyes grew wide and all the colour drained from her face. "Chapman? Miss Chapman?"

"Do you need a chair?" Fritz asked as he looked for the nearest place to place a lady who looked as if she were about to swoon. However, Miss Wesley seemed to not hear him. Her wide eyes were locked on Belle.

"Belle, this is Miss Wesley. Miss Wesley, Miss Chapman. I am her grandfather's physician," he explained to Belle.

"Do you have a brother?" Miss Wesley asked.

"Yes, I have two – Sidney and Miles."

Fritz caught Miss Wesley when her knees collapsed as if they lacked the strength to stand. "A chair," he barked to Walter who had joined them. "Miss Wesley needs a chair."

"No, no, I will be well as soon as I am somewhere other than here."

"You will sit down," Fritz commanded. "Your grandfather would not wish for me to allow you to roam away when your legs cannot support you while standing. Why think of the trouble you could find yourself in if you were to stumble and fall." He steered her toward a chair that Walter had pulled closer to where they were standing but not away from the wall where it would impede the movement of the mingling crowd.

"I cannot stay here," Miss Wesley protested.

"Do you know one of my brothers?" Belle knelt beside Miss Wesley and held her hand.

"Yes, she does. Charlotte, are you well?" A gentleman pushed past Fritz.

"Miss Wesley," Miss Wesley ground out through gritted teeth. "You must call me Miss Wesley, Mr. Chapman, and Mr. Norman has already seen to my care. *You* are not needed."

"Miles?" Belle said as she rose. "What are you doing here? Are you not supposed to be at school?"

He shrugged. "School is dull."

"School is important," Belle replied.

"Very," Miss Wesley agreed.

"For those who need to find a profession, it is paramount," Miles agreed. He turned toward Fritz. "Norman is it?"

Fritz swallowed. "Yes."

"*The* Mr. Norman?" He glanced at Belle before turning his eyes back to Fritz.

"If you mean the best physician in Bath who is well-loved by many, then, yes," Walter inserted.

The man was standing close enough to Fritz that he could feel the front of Walter's jacket touching his shoulder. Some men might find a friend's unrequested assistance to be insulting, but not Fritz. He was currently too much in shock to say much.

Belle stepped around her brother and laced her fingers with Fritz's. "Yes, Miles, this is my Mr. Norman." Then, after smiling at Fritz, she lifted his hand to her lips and kissed it before repeating to Fritz while looking into his eyes, "My Mr. Norman."

Chapter 14

Her brother's smile did not falter at her declaration that Fritz was hers. In fact, it seemed to grow from curious to absolutely delighted.

"Father does not know Mr. Norman is in Bath, does he?"

Was it not possible for her brother to ever look anything but completely at ease and as if everything that entered his life was a lark? He was supposed to be shocked, not pleased, and he was to sound suspicious and possibly angry, not as if he were about to erupt in peals of laughter.

"No, he does not," Aunt Augusta inserted, "and it shall remain that way."

Miles looked momentarily surprised which was somewhat satisfying to Belle.

"It is a pleasure to see you, Miles."

"Likewise, Aunt, and you may rest assured that

I have no intention of alerting Father to my being anywhere near Bath."

"It is good to know you have more sense than my brother," Aunt Augusta said.

"That is no challenge," Miles muttered as a very rare thing, a frown, touched his lips. Belle had seen him pout when younger and feign displeasure a few times when he was older, but she rarely saw Miles frown. The sight of it made her quite curious as to its source.

"I think that Mr. Wesley might like to have his granddaughter returned to him," she said to Fritz. "And while you are seeing to that, I shall see to my brother."

"But I had wanted to –" Miles began.

"This is best," Belle interrupted him. "Miss Wesley needs rest, and Mr. Norman, being her grandfather's physician, is the best person to inform him of her need." She held Miles's gaze. He was not one to be easily persuaded away from his purpose because he was used to getting his way. However, he was not going to succeed in having his way if she could prevent it.

For a second time in the space of two minutes, her youngest brother startled her. This time by remaining silent and giving a sharp nod of acceptance, and with only a word of concern for Miss Wesley to which he received an assurance that she would be well, he allowed Fritz to assist the lady to her feet. He, then, stood back and watch as Miss Wesley and Fritz began their journey to the other side of the room. There was no smile on his face. There was no ease to his manner. Concern etched his features, and the muscles of his jaw flexed and then relaxed several times. Apparently, he did possess the ability to approach some things as if they were not a lark.

"May I introduce you to my friends?" Belle asked, drawing Miles's attention away from Miss Wesley.

"Certainly." His smile was back, but it seemed to lack its normal brilliance.

"This is Mr. Blakesley and his wife, Mrs. Blakesley. Next to them are Mr. and Mrs. Clayton. Mrs. Clayton is Mrs. Blakesley's cousin. And then, we have Mr. and Mrs. Shelton. These three gentlemen are good friends and attended school together." She allowed an eyebrow to arch as she looked at her brother while saying the word school.

"And we are all good friends of Mr. Norman,"

Mr. Shelton inserted. "Blakesley more than the rest of us, but none of us would not abide any harm coming to him."

Belle had not known the Sheltons or the Claytons for very long. However, from the beginning of her acquaintance with them, she had found them to be some of the best sorts of people, and Mr. Shelton's comment now solidified him as someone whom she wished to always call her friend.

"I am not here to do Mr. Norman any harm," Miles assured Mr. Shelton. "I am here to see Miss Wesley and clear up a misunderstanding." He closed his eyes for a moment and his face pinched as if he did not wish to admit to something. Then, upon opening his eyes, he added, "And I had hoped to gain an audience with Mr. Norman."

"You did?" Belle asked in surprise.

He nodded.

"Why?"

Miles darted a look around them before answering softly. "I read one of his letters which are passed from physician to physician and wished to know more on the topic."

Belle blinked. Why would her brother wish to know more about some medical topic?

"I will explain later," he assured her. "So long as you promise not to mention a word of any of this to Father." He flinched at the name.

Something very interesting was afoot. Miles never grimaced at the mention of their father. He was the favoured child. He could do no wrong and, therefore, had been blessed with no need to think ill of their father.

Belle followed his gaze as it shifted away from him. He was watching Miss Wesley. That young lady must have something to do with the changes in her brother.

"You will stay with me, will you not?" Aunt Augusta asked.

Miles shook his head. "I have already taken a room for a few days. I had not planned to be in Bath long."

"Had you even planned to call on me at all?" Aunt Augusta gave him one of her most withering looks, which, in true Miles fashion, caused him to laugh instead of cowering.

"Indeed, I had, but not until after I had seen Mr. Norman and Miss Wesley, of course."

"Relegated to last on the list, am I?"

Again, instead of being cowed by their aunt's displeasure, Miles laughed. "The dessert of social calls, which everyone who is anyone knows are the best – delicious morsels left to savour at the conclusion of the main purpose of being in an area."

Aunt Augusta pursed her lips and arched a skeptical eyebrow. "Your pretty words will not work on me, young man."

Miles sobered. "Very well, I had hoped to discover if Mr. Norman had seen Belle, and if he had not yet called on her, I wished to encourage it." He shrugged. "There it is. I have said it. That was my other purpose in wishing to see Mr. Norman. However, it seems my assistance was not – is not – needed in that area."

Belle's brow furrowed. "You were going to speak to Fritz on my behalf?"

Miles sighed. "I do not wish to discuss all of this here."

"Then, allow me to call for my carriage, and we will retire to my house."

"Aunt," Belle said, glancing at Grace without saying anything further.

Her aunt huffed. "I was going to invite the whole lot of us to find a cup of tea and a morsel of food at my home, but I suppose we should not make a grand exit as it will set too many tongues wagging. However, I am not the patient sort, I will have you know."

"We will exit in pieces," Mr. Shelton whispered. "Grace and Blakesley will dance while Vic and I make a show of taking a tour of the card room. Clayton can escort his wife to the corridor to get some air, and Miss Chapman must remain to make a statement by dancing a second set with Norman."

Aunt Augusta's eyebrows shot up. "That was a hastily formed plan, and a rather good one, Mr. Shelton."

Mr. Shelton thanked her while Mr. Clayton chuckled.

"One can always count on Shelton for a quick plan of escape," Mr. Clayton said. "He has had plenty of practice."

"For as long as I have known him," Mrs. Shelton agreed. "And we met as children," she added to Miles.

"I think that you could enter a group," Mr. Shelton said to Belle. "Norman is nearly here. Go meet him and dance. We will meet you near the carriage door." He tipped his head toward the dance floor. "Go."

Belle did not wait for a second reminder. She made her way to the dance floor and steered Fritz into formation with some other dancers. "Aunt Augusta would like to retire early," she said by way of explaining why they could not wait until another dance but must join this one.

"Is she well?" Fritz's eyes darted toward where her aunt stood.

"She is," she said and then mouthed, "Miles."

His eyes went wide for a moment before he nodded his understanding.

They made their way through the dance with little talking, but it did not matter that they were silent. They did not always need to speak to converse with one another. A lingering look, a soft squeeze of her hand, the contented smile on Fritz's lips were enough to mark this dance, their last before they married, as a dear and precious memory for Belle.

When the dance concluded, Fritz lifted Belle's hand to his lips before tucking it in the crook of his arm and leading her to where her aunt stood near the door to the ballroom.

~*~*~

Three-quarters of an hour later, Aunt Augusta's drawing room was filled with people eager to hear what Miles had to say.

Belle was pleased to see her younger brother looking somewhat flustered. If he was going to leave school and make an appearance in Bath without so much as a letter saying he was coming, he deserved to feel a bit of trepidation, and she was happy to see that he did.

"I had not thought I would be sharing this with so many," he began.

"Then, you should have called on me before making an appearance at the Upper Rooms."

Miles inclined his head in acceptance of his aunt's reprimand. "Where shall I begin?" He tapped his lip with a finger.

"Might I suggest you begin with why you are not at school," Belle offered. "And do not tell me because it is dull. I suspected there is more to it than that."

Her comment was met with a nod. "There is."

He paused. "Not a word of this can reach our father."

"None of us will tell him anything," she assured him. She knew that look of fear in his eyes. She had felt it six years ago and still felt it now as she waited to marry Fritz. Their father had a way of inserting himself where he was not wanted.

"I have always been my father's favourite," he explained to the others. "I never had to fear that he would deny me anything." He blew out a breath. "That is until a month ago. I was at a soiree, which was not an unusual place for me to be. School mattered little. Father was going to provide for me. I may be his third-born son, but I would not be required to take up a profession. I would be given a small piece of land with a house and fields, as well as a sizable fortune – equal in amount to my sisters' dowries."

Mr. Shelton whistled softly, and Miles nodded his head.

"Indeed, it was a lovely arrangement. The only requirement was to be what my father expected me to be – a self-indulgent fop who presented a pretty picture which would cause one and all to admire Sir Allen better." Miles shook his head. "It seemed easy enough, and it was enjoyable, for the most part."

"However..." Mr. Clayton said.

"Ah, yes, however," Miles agreed. "That pretty picture which I was to paint did not include courting a mere gentleman's daughter with no significant connections and whose ties to the land were not ancient. Father is not above doing his due diligence in discovering the background of any lady or gentleman," he gave Fritz a sad smile, "who presents him or herself as a potential match for his children – even his favourite son. I thought nothing of it at first. I assumed that father would allow me to have what I wished just as he always had." He shook his head. "Yes, I know exactly how that sounds, and I am ashamed I have been so arrogant."

"Father does not approve of Miss Wesley?"

He shook his head in reply to Belle's question.

"What did he do?" A small, familiar panic began to flutter in her breast, and she took Fritz's hand to assure herself that he was there and there was no need to be anxious for herself.

"He wrote her a letter pretending to be me, breaking off our courtship – informal as it was, by telling her all the ways in which she was unacceptable to me."

His revelation was met with a collective gasp.

"Any chance I had of convincing her that I was not a shallow and vain fellow – which I was, but which I had also been attempting not to be – was gone. We spoke once after she received *my* letter, or I should say, she spoke, and I listened in dumbfounded horror. Then, she fled the area to visit her grandparents." He closed his eyes again. "There are rumors that began when she made her hasty exit."

"Oh, do not say it!" Grace cried.

He smiled at her. "I will not. They are too despicable."

"Was your name attached to those rumors?" Fritz asked.

Miles shook his head. "Whoever started them –"

"Father," Belle inserted. "He made certain your name would not be tarnished."

"Precisely."

"Did you speak to him about this?"

"No. I knew by then that it would do no good. I have been with him when he has instructed Sidney about the requirements for being his heir." He shook his head. "And I knew what he had done to you." Again, his head shook from side to side as if everything was too horrible to even consider. "I find myself in need of a profession, for, I will not allow Father to tarnish Miss Wesley's name. I have come to present the situation to her and her grandparents before I go speak to her father."

"You intend to marry her?" Mr. Blakesley asked.

"The rumors have not reached Bath. However, if Father should discover I was here..."

"Does she know of these rumors at all?"

He shrugged. "Only if her parents have heard, which is possible." He scrubbed his face with his hands. "I doubt she will like my solution, but I must offer it."

"Do you love her?" Fritz asked.

Miles shrugged and then nodded. "I believe I do."

"But without a profession, how will you provide for her?" Aunt Augusta asked.

Miles shrank into himself. "I do not know. I must find something to do. I have a bit of money saved – not as much as I should, but I am not penniless."

"Were you coming to me for a loan?" his aunt asked.

"I had thought about it, but I did not wish to come without a plan." He turned to Fritz. "That was why I had hoped to speak with you – well about that and to beg forgiveness for my father's actions and urge you to call on Belle."

"You were going to do that?" Fritz asked in surprise.

"I was, and I was hopeful that you might help point me in the right direction for a profession. You see, I have always found the science of the body and its health fascinating. I have read much about the improvements in treatments of various ailments. I have studied in detail the tinctures and tonics of the apothecary, as well as the workings of our bodies."

"You wish to be a physician?" Belle could not contain her surprise. She knew that Miles had always been an inquisitive child when the apothecary or surgeon had paid a call, but she would never have thought he would consider being a physician. She was well aware of what her father thought of physicians. They were beneath him and his family.

Miles shook his head. "I do not think I would make a good one. While I enjoy learning about the body and treatments and the like, I am deplorable when faced with the unpleasantness of an illness or injury. However, I have found while at school, that I enjoy researching and writing. If I could find a way to combine these two areas of interest in a useful fashion... I had hoped Mr. Norman might have some suggestions."

Belle looked at Fritz whose brow was furrowed. He tipped his head one way and then another.

"You have published many letters," Miles continued. "I could compile them into a volume for you and with you."

"And profit from the publication?" Mr. Blakesley asked.

"Yes."

"I already have an assistant."

"But you do not have a research assistant or a secretary."

"A secretary!" Belle cried. "You wish to be a secretary?"

"I do."

"No wonder you do not wish for Father to know about this."

Miles nodded. "Especially considering to whom I hope to attach myself."

"Why me?" Fritz asked.

One of Miles's shoulders lifted and lowered in a half-shrug. "For two reasons. First, Belle loves you, which means you are of good character, and second, you are well-known for your writing. I am certain I could learn much from you."

"What do you think, Blakesley?" Fritz asked.

"It is not an unworthy idea. I would give it consideration."

"And you, Belle, what do you think?"

Belle looked at her youngest brother. "Are you intent upon breaking ties with Father?"

"What choice do I have! I cannot allow him to harm Miss Wesley."

"But what if she does not accept your offer?" Belle asked.

Miles swallowed. "I want nothing to do with a man who would do such things to others. I was too young to do anything when he separated you from Mr. Norman, and I was far too self-absorbed to understand it. However, I am no longer so young, and I understand the heinousness of his actions too well now. I cannot be what he wants me to be. I must be something different – even if it is not as

Miss Wesley's husband or through working with Mr. Norman."

"I will consider it," Fritz said. He squeezed Belle's hand. "I will look at our finances and consider it."

Chapter 15

Two days later, Fritz paced in the back of the church as he waited for his and Belle's time with the parson. Belle had not yet arrived. If she were here, he was certain he would find it easier to just wait calmly for their appointment.

"She will be here," Walter assured him in a whisper so as to not disturb the ceremony which was nearing its conclusion at the front of the church. Grace was to arrive with Belle and Mrs. King. So, currently, it was just Walter who stood with Fritz awaiting the arrival of their guests and the bride.

"I cannot help being anxious." He blew out a breath and willed himself to stand still. He checked his watch. Ten minutes. She *had* to be here before ten minutes was up.

The door opened and Fritz's heart picked up its

pace only to be disappointed when it was not Belle who entered.

"Belle is on her way," Miles said. "I stopped at Aunt Augusta's before coming here. However, we may have a problem."

"Explain," Walter rumbled softly, but then waited silently as the parson prayed and concluded the wedding taking place.

Fritz nodded a greeting to the Sheltons and Claytons as they entered. This would be the extent of the wedding guests both here at the church and afterward at the wedding breakfast.

"I had forgotten my gift for Belle," Miles explained, keeping his voice low, "and when I went to retrieve it from my rented room, my father's carriage was outside."

"He is in Bath?" Could a man's heart thump harder than Fritz's currently was? Fritz was not certain it could, and, over the years, he placed his ear against several hearts which were beating far faster than they should.

Miles nodded. "He is looking for me."

"Did you show yourself to him?" Mr. Shelton asked.

"No, should I have?"

Mr. Shelton crossed his arms and glowered at Miles. "Where do you think he will go when he cannot find you?"

Miles looked as if he was going to be ill as he grasped what his error had been.

"If she is not here in two minutes," Walter said to Fritz, "I will go get her."

"We," Miles said. "*We* will go get her." He ran a hand through his hair. "I only thought of how much I did not wish to see him." He looked at Fritz apologetically.

"That is understandable. I would not – do not – wish to see him either," Fritz assured him. "I remember making exits through corridors and doors that most did not use to avoid your father six years ago. He can be quite unpleasant."

He sucked in a deep breath and released it. The anxious fluttering in his stomach and the beating of his heart calmed. Things were not now what they had been six years ago. What truly did he have to fear with friends such as he had surrounding him at present? He would marry Belle today, or they would be off to Scotland. Belle was his. He would not let her go again.

Thankfully, within a minute of Walter marking the time on his watch, Belle and Grace arrived.

"Aunt Augusta said to go on without her if she does not arrive shortly after I do," Belle said after a quick greeting for Fritz. "Father is looking for you," she added, turning to her brother. "When Grace and I were sneaking out the servants' entrance, Aunt Augusta was telling him that the place to be seen by anyone of importance whether young or old was the Pump Room, so that would be a good place to begin a search. With any luck, Father is on his way there now."

Fritz sighed silently in relief. Mrs. King was clever. It would take Sir Allen a great deal of time to discover if Miles was at the Pump Room, for a man such as Sir Allen, who lived to be seen and admired, would not be able to resist the need to parade himself through those gathered. While he knew he would marry Belle despite whatever her father might do, he also did not relish the idea of the scene which the man would cause if he arrived at the church before or even during the ceremony.

"I will see if we can begin a minute or two early," Walter said, before making his way to the front of the church as the couple whose ceremony had just finished was preparing to leave with those who had attended as witnesses to the blessed event.

"Belle," Miles offered her his arm. "May I escort you to the front?"

Belle looked at Fritz, who nodded.

"You should go take your place then so that Miles can bring me to you." Despite the somewhat ominous air which hung over them, her smile was filled with nothing but joy and peace.

How fortunate he was to be loved by such a lady as she was! Wearing a smile of his own that he felt throughout his entire person, Fritz did as Belle suggested, with the Claytons and Sheltons following behind him.

"We will wait just a moment for Aunt Augusta" Miles called to them. "But only a moment," he said when Fritz looked back at him.

How was it that the ticks of a clock seemed to fly by when one was attempting to discern the best treatment plan for an injured or ill patient, but when one was anticipating the culmination of six years of waiting to marry the lady one loved, as Fritz was, those ticks seemed to be separated by great gulfs of time? It was surely one of the greatest mysteries of the universe.

However, even when perceptually altered by impatience, time did move forward, and just as Fritz was taking his place at the front with Walter, Mrs. King – and only Mrs. King – arrived, and Belle, with her aunt on one side and her brother on the other, made her way to take her place at his side, where she would always be from this day forward.

Delight far greater than he had even imagined he would feel at this moment filled Fritz as he took Belle's hand while the parson began reading the well-known words of the wedding ceremony. In what seemed to Fritz to be only a matter of moments, the entire service had been read, the register had been signed, and he and Belle had made their way to Walter's small carriage which was waiting to take them to the wedding breakfast.

The top of the carriage had been removed, and there were ribbons attached to the sides, as well as a few flowers along with more ribbons, on Lady, who stood, waiting for Fritz to give the command to walk on. Fritz helped Belle into the vehicle, and then, after climbing up himself, he pulled her to her feet and into his embrace.

Walter held the reins and ensured the carriage

stayed where it should while Belle laughed and Mr. Shelton and Mr. Clayton huzzahed. And Fritz? Fritz took in the joy around him with a glance before giving his wife — *his wife* — a kiss, which like the decorations on the carriage and horse was the sort that would let one and all who witnessed it know that he was no longer a single man.

~*~*~

"We were beginning to wonder if you were going to join us," Mr. Shelton teased when Belle and Fritz arrived at Mrs. King's home.

"There were several who wanted to wish joy to the best doctor in Bath," Belle explained.

With each stop to shake a hand or to tip his hat to whoever called to him, Fritz had taken the opportunity to kiss his wife. He should be shocked at his behaviour as it was far from what was considered proper, but he found it impossible to feel anything but delight. There would be absolutely no one in Bath, whether that person was a temporary resident for the season, one who remained all year, or a baronet who was only passing through town looking for his son, who would not know that he and Miss Chapman were married and very happily so. Scandalous it might be to kiss one's wife so publicly and repeatedly. However, it was also a way, according to Belle who had suggested the plan, to ensure that her father could not try some scheme to part them without knowing that his daughter's reputation would be in tatters, and a daughter with a tattered reputation would reflect very poorly on her father.

"As well they should," Mrs. King said proudly. "Now, shall we all go in and have a feast?" She motioned for Fritz and Belle to lead them into the dining room.

No sooner had they gotten seated than there was a commotion in the entryway.

"Augusta! What is the meaning of this?" Sir Allen's look was severe as he examined the dining room.

"It is a wedding breakfast," Mrs. King replied calmly. "It is not polite to shout in the house. Father would be shocked."

"Father is long dead," Sir Allen replied.

"If you can keep your voice down, you may join us. I shall have a place set for you directly."

"What do you mean this is a wedding breakfast?"

"Do you wish to join us?" Mrs. King answered.

"I wish to know what is going on!"

"I shall not answer you when you are shouting," Mrs. King nodded to a footman. "Pay him no mind, John, we are awaiting our feast."

With a wary look at Sir Allen, John began placing food in front of each person. Fritz was positive he would not be able to eat with Sir Allen glowering at him from the doorway to the dining room.

Mrs. King smiled at her brother. "Since you have decided to remain silent, I will tell you what we are celebrating, though I am certain anyone with eyes and a partially working mind could have figured it out without explanation. Belle and Mr. Norman have married, and we are celebrating their union." She ate a spoonful of soup. "Are you certain you do not wish for a plate?"

"Mr. Norman?" His eyes narrowed as he glared at Fritz.

"Yes. Mr. Norman. Bath's most well-respected and sought-after physician," Mrs. King said as she lifted her cup of tea to her lips.

To Fritz, it was impressive how coolly she was responding to the obviously furious Sir Allen.

"You would do well to treat him kindly if you

wish to retain your good name," she added. "I am not exaggerating when I say he has connections whom you would not wish to think ill of you."

One eyebrow arched as his glare moved from Fritz to his sister. "And who are *these* people?" he asked with a wave of his hand. "Friends of Mr. Norman?"

Mrs. King nodded. "Indeed, they are, as are half the population of Bath."

Sir Allen snorted derisively, but it did not fluster Mrs. King.

"Shall I begin introductions with the highest rank?"

"Is there any other way?" her brother's tone was mocking.

"The gentleman on my left, seated next to his wife at the far end of the table, is Mr. Clayton."

"Why is he at the end of the table if he is of highest rank?"

"Because Blakesley is a particular friend of Mrs. King," Mr. Clayton replied.

Sir Allen huffed. "You cannot be of any great rank if you allow such things."

"His father is Sir Herbert Clayton of Stratsbury

Park," Belle said, drawing her father's attention. "I believe that baronetcy is in your book, is it not?"

His eyes narrowed as he nodded.

"Mr. Clayton shall, one day, become Sir Graeme," Belle added.

"I see," was all her father said.

"Also, at the far end of the table, but on the right, is Mr. Shelton and his wife," Mrs. King continued the introductions.

"Mr. Shelton is the heir to his father's estate which is of notable size," Belle inserted.

Fritz could not help but admire the way his wife gave just that bit of additional information which she knew her father would find hard to discredit.

"And on my left, are Mr. and Mrs. Blakesley. It was Mr. Blakesley who helped me find this house. He has very good taste, does he not?" Mrs. King asked.

"Indeed, he does," Belle assured her before her father could say a word. "There are many who rely on Mr. Blakesley to help them find accommodations. Mr. Shelton and Mr. Clayton, both of whom are great friends of Mr. Blakesley and attended college together, are leasing Mr. Blakesley's estate, Erondale, for the season. Mr.

and Mrs. Blakesley have a residence in Bath that is a little smaller than this one but is just as elegant."

"I also count Norman as my dearest friend," Walter added. "And, I am not above sharing my displeasure with anyone who should ask, and even those who should not ask, if you were to attempt anything to harm him again."

Sir Allen's eyes grew a wide at the directly and forcefully stated comment.

"Neither would I," Mr. Clayton said.

"I am no stranger to causing a stir," Mr. Shelton added by way of support.

To Fritz, the scene unfolding before him was in stark contrast to six years ago when those he had trusted began to worry about their own positions and suggested that he find another place to practice his profession.

Sir Allen's lips pursed, and his jaw clenched as he studied Belle. "You are married?" he asked after a minute of scrutiny.

"Yes," she replied with a smile. "Finally."

"I shall not receive you," he said.

"I do not care if you do," Belle said with a lift of her chin.

"Nor will your mother or sisters or brothers."

"At least, not while you live," Miles muttered. "And, Belle, I am not part of those relations, I shall receive you with pleasure."

Fritz could see Sir Allen begin to seethe at the comment and decided it was time for him to speak. "Imagine what will be said about you when people learn that you have cast your daughter aside," he said. "The population of Bath is not always in Bath. They travel back to their homes and to London. Some return regularly, some do not."

"You would not."

Mr. Shelton chuckled. "No, he would not because Norman is far too good. I, however, am not."

For a long silent, heavy moment, it looked as if Sir Allen was going to make a protest, but he did not. Instead, he turned to Miles. "Come along, son. We have things to discuss about your future."

"About that," Mrs. King inserted, "Miles will be returning to school to complete his course of study, which you will pay for, of course, for if you do not, questions will be raised and answers will be given." She held his gaze without wavering. "Then, I believe, he is returning to Bath to take up a position as a research assistant to Mr. Norman."

She looked at Fritz for confirmation. "And should fortune shine on him, when he returns, we will have another feast to celebrate his wedding."

"You will not marry—"

"I will if she will accept me," Miles retorted before his father could finish his directive.

"You will not receive a farthing of what I have set aside for you if you do."

"I know."

The simple reply seemed to startle Sir Allen more than anything had done to this point.

"Do you wish for a plate?" Mrs. King asked again with a bat of her lashes.

"No! I want no part of *anything* that is here." He gave each of his children a pointed look before turning and leaving.

"That was most unpleasant," Mr. Shelton said.

"He is the biggest fool I have ever met." Mrs. King shook her head. "I am not sorry to see him go, but I am sorry for his children."

"And his wife," Belle said softly.

"Yes, and your mother." She patted Belle's hand. "You may take your wife to the sitting room, Mr. Norman. She may look calm, but she cannot possibly be in any state to eat at present."

Thanking her, Fritz rose, took Belle by the hand, and left the room.

"I am well. Truly, I am," Belle assured him as they entered the sitting room.

"Are you?" He pulled her into his embrace. He doubted it very much and let his tone carry his misgivings.

"I will be."

In response, he simply rubbed her back and held her.

"I knew he would be angry and disagreeable, but I admit to being somewhat hurt regardless."

"I would be concerned if you were not." He pulled back and smiled at her. "Do you have any regrets?"

She shook her head as a brilliant smile spread across her face. "How can I regret marrying the man I love more than anything in this world?" She gave him a quick kiss. "And do we not have the best friends?"

Fritz's head bobbed up and down emphatically as he said, "Indeed, we do!"

"Then, our life is just as it should be." She cupped his cheek with her right hand. "What life does not contain some sorrow?"

"I wish yours did not," Fritz admitted.

"Not even you can prevent or cure all that is ill in the world."

"I suppose you are correct, though I wish I could – for you." His hand cradled the back of her head as his other one held her firmly to him.

"Kiss me often, love me always, and I shall be the happiest creature in the world."

A laugh, light and refreshing, bubbled out of him. "That, my darling Belle, I can do." And with that, he claimed her lips and spoke to her without words of his great and undying love for her, his one and only, irreplaceable Belle.

Before You Go

If you enjoyed this book, be sure to let others know by leaving a review.

~*~*~

Want to know when other books in this series will be available?

You can always know what's new with my books by subscribing to my mailing list.

(There will, of course, be a thank you gift for joining because I think my readers are awesome!)

Book News from Leenie Brown

(bit.ly/LeenieBBookNews)

~*~*~

Turn the page to read an excerpt of another one of Leenie's books

Other Pens, Mansfield Park Excerpt

[Have you ever wondered what happened to Henry Crawford after *Mansfield Park* ended? How about his sister or Tom Bertram? What about his friends who were never at Mansfield Park? If you have wondered about such things, you'll want to read my *Other Pens, Mansfield Park* series, which mixes Jane Austen's classic characters with a cast of original ones in situations never found in one of Miss Austen's novels. Below is an excerpt from the second book in the series, *Charles: To Discover His Purpose*, a story about how Henry Crawford's rakish friend Charles Edwards finds his happily ever after while attempting to steal a kiss.]

CHAPTER 1

Charles Edwards squinted into the late afternoon

sun – it was an action that he could almost do without any discomfort. The swelling around his eye had subsided, and soon, the bruising would fade to a nasty yellow and then disappear. Until that happened, he would continue to take his rides by wandering from one street to the next rather than face the taunting and questioning looks he was guaranteed to receive in the parks.

While it was an excellent way to avoid censure from his peers, it was dashed boring trotting up and down streets without so much as a single friend with whom to converse. Had he earned his scars more gallantly, perhaps he would not feel the need to hide them. To have been injured in a boxing match or defense of some lady's honor would make his bruises more of a badge than a blemish. However, since everyone in town had likely read that blasted article in the paper, the raised eyebrows from overprotective matrons and giggles from their charges would be unbearable. And then, there would be the gentlemen. He shook his head. Had he received a blackened eye from Trefor Linton for actually doing something inappropriate with Linton's sister, Constance, his friends would just laugh and clap him on the shoulder before filling his glass with some libation at his club.

But, he had not been caught doing anything improper. In fact, it was much worse than just not being found dallying with a debutante. He had been attempting to be gallant. He would do his best not to be put in such a situation again! Honourable actions and favours to ladies who were offering none in return must be avoided, for they only led to broken noses, disgrace, and lonely rambles up less well-to-do streets.

"Mr. Edwards?"

Charles drew his horse to a stop just in front of a carriage that was standing at the ready to receive a lovely young woman. He had not bothered to take note of her since this was not the part of town where the finest flowers of the season resided.

"Miss Linton," he said doffing his hat. "Is Crawford with you?" He nodded to the carriage.

"No," Constance Linton replied with a smile, "though he very much wanted to be. It is just Evelyn and I."

His brows furrowed. Evelyn? The name sounded familiar.

"Miss Barrett," Constance clarified.

"Ah, Miss Barrett. Of course. How negligent of me to not remember." How had he managed to forget her name? He certainly had not forgotten her perfectly pink lips or lithe figure...the same figure that was exiting the house to his left. She was perhaps the most enticing creature he had ever met and never sampled.

"Oh!"

Miss Barrett's lips formed such a wonderfully kissable o.

"Mr. Edwards," she greeted with a small curtsey. "Are you here to visit Mrs. Verity and the children?"

His brows furrowed again. "Mrs. Who?"

"Verity," Evelyn repeated. "She runs this home for children." She motioned toward the house.

"I did not know this was a home for children." His left brow rose in question. "Why are you here? None of these children are yours, I would assume."

Her eyes grew wide, and she gasped. "We are not all as reprobate as you, Mr. Edwards."

He leaned forward, nonchalantly admiring her look of utter indignation. "Then, what, pray tell, are proper young ladies such as yourself and Miss Linton doing here?"

"Charitable work. You do know what that is, do you not?"

He chuckled. Miss Barret was not the sort to shy away quietly to her corner and leave him be. He liked that. "I have heard the term."

"But have you ever experienced it?" asked Constance.

He shifted his gaze to his friend, Henry Crawford's, betrothed. "No, not beyond what is expected on my father's estate."

"It's rather fulfilling," Constance replied. "Today, we taught some children their letters. It was remarkable, was it not, Evelyn?" She wore a look of sheer delight.

"And Linton approves of this?" Charles asked.

"Both he and Henry do."

Delight did not begin to describe the look in Miss Linton's eyes as she said the name Henry. One day, when he was ready to take up his mantle of responsibility, Charles hoped to find a lady who would look even half as happy saying his name as Miss Linton did at this moment.

"Trefor," Constance continued, "thought this would be a safe way to keep me occupied. My last scheme, you see, did not leave him favourably disposed to allowing me to find ways in which to make my life more interesting."

There was a mischievous gleam in both her eyes and those of her friend Evelyn. Curious, that. He had not expected anything akin to impishness from Trefor Linton's sister or any of her friends. Constance Linton was the most proper chit he had ever met, and he suspected, to be her friend, Miss Barrett must be the same.

"Is your eye feeling better?" Miss Barrett asked.

"It is, but I'll not be doing either of you any favours in the future," he replied with a smirk. "At least not unless I receive something better than a broken nose and a black eye in return."

"I can neither apologize or thank you enough," Constance replied.

She had apologized over and over and over again as she stood holding a compress to his eye in the Linton sitting room those many days ago. "I think you have said the words enough," he replied softly. "I merely jest." He would not have her feeling guilty for his injuries when it was not her doing which caused them.

Miss Barrett tipped her head as she looked up at him, a puzzled look on her face. Then, she shook herself and smiled. "We are expected at your house soon, Connie. Mother will be waiting."

"As will Trefor," she smiled, "and Henry."

Much to Charles's surprise, Miss Evelyn Barrett rolled her eyes at the tone her friend used to say Henry's name.

"Do not let me detain you. I would not wish to run afoul of any of them." He winked at Miss Barret. "At least, not until I am healed."

She gasped. "My mother has warned me about you, Mr. Edwards."

"As well she should," he replied easily. "I am dreadfully charming."

Constance had entered the carriage, but Evelyn, who remained on the street, laughed. "That is not how my mother said it." Her eyes sparkled with impertinence. Then, with a small curtsey of parting, she boarded her carriage.

Charles looked after her and tipped his hat as the door closed on those shining eyes and teasing smile. Oh, he could find great pleasure in evoking such a look from her on a regular basis. Not that he wished to spend great amounts of time with her. No, he was not the sort of gentleman to trot around behind a lady hoping for her to smile at him or laugh at his jokes. He danced; he flirted; and he stole kisses. He did not become attached. Attachments were dangerous. They led to marriage and, he fought the urge to shudder, responsibility. He was far too young for such things as that just yet.

Still, he wondered where she would be this evening and if there would be any dark corners into which she might be persuaded.

He blew out a breath. Hiding himself away from society was perhaps not the best idea in the world. It apparently was wreaking havoc on his well-ordered, carefree existence. A rogue such as himself did not stalk his prey. He simply looked for the opportunity and took it. Planning anything was far too much like being responsible. Rules, guidelines, ledgers, accounts, and all the rest that went with being a gentleman of standing belonged to his father, not Charles.

In front of him, the carriage stopped, a man jumped down, the door opened, and a pretty face peered out, looking back to where he was.

He nudged his horse forward as Miss Barrett waved him towards her.

"Do you require help?" he asked as he drew near.

"No, no, we are well. Connie and I were just talking, and I thought as we were discussing how dreadful it is that you were injured on Connie's account that it would be charitable of us to offer you a place in the Linton's box at the theatre tonight."

Charles began to shake his head.

"Hear me out. Do not refuse until I have made my full request. And come forward more, I feel as if I am going to fall out of this door and onto the street."

Charles chuckled. This young woman sounded more like Linton's cantankerous Aunt Gwladys than a young lady of the ton. Most young ladies who presented themselves during the season went out of their way to appear demure to one and all – always.

"Do you scold everyone?" he teased as he did as she said.

If he had expected her to be offended, he was once again going to be surprised, for she merely smiled, batted her lashes, and replied, "No, I scold very few beyond my brother actually."

"So, I am special," he returned.

She shrugged. "Perhaps you are. Or perhaps I just find you as troublesome as Griffin."

"I think I will insist you find me special."

"Do what you will; it matters not one jot to me," she retorted.

Her words might have said she did not care, but her tone clearly said she was annoyed.

"As I was saying..."

"Before you began scolding." Charles smiled at her huff.

"Before I had to pause to give instructions."

Charles chuckled. "Continue. I shall not refuse until you have said your piece."

"Refuse? You intend to refuse?"

"Most likely. But, I have not heard your request in full, so I cannot be certain I am correct until I do. I have been wrong before."

Her brows rose, and her lips pursed for a moment as if she were holding back some retort.

"There will not be very many people in our box. If you slip in a side door or something and scurry up to the box, you will not have to have many people gawk at you."

"You think I am worried about being seen?"

"I would be if my eye were the colour of yours.

That *is* why you are riding here and not in a more populated place, is it not? And, I have not seen you at any events since...well..." she pointed to her eye.

"I will admit that I do not relish the whispers." Why he felt he needed to admit such a thing was beyond him. He could come up with any number of reasons to be riding where he was and for not having been at any soiree she had attended. A smile slipped slowly across his face. "Have you missed me?"

"What?" She shook her head vigorously. "No. I just noticed that I had not seen you slinking from shadow to shadow."

"If you say so."

"I do." She scowled. "Now, will you be joining us? I am certain no one would be in the least put out if you did."

"How reassuring," Charles muttered.

"Please," Constance added from the interior of the carriage. "I do feel dreadful that you have been out of society. It must be terribly boring sitting at home instead of going out."

"Who said I was sitting at home?" He smiled a lazy, suggestive smile.

"Henry," Constance replied.

Blast! Did Henry tell her everything?

"Very well, I have been hiding away. Are you happy to know my shame?"

"Only if it means you will join us," said Miss Barrett.

"Can you not muster an ounce of sympathy?" he asked in surprise. Were not young ladies – especially those who did charity work – supposed to be compassionate?

She shook her head. "No. Not a morsel. While I am awfully sorry you were injured, I do believe you have escaped more times than you have been caught."

The lady might look like an angel, but she had a heart of ice. However, ice could be melted. In fact, it could be quite a marvelous lark to attempt to melt that ice.

"Very well, I will join you if you will but attempt to feel an ounce of pity for me."

The way her lips pursed with contained amusement was tempting. "A full ounce?"

"Yes." He moved closer to her door. "A full ounce." He repeated the words in a low, sultry tone – slowly and deliberately. Satisfaction curled his lips as he saw her pretty nibble-worthy neck rise and fall when she swallowed.

She licked her lips. "I shall make an attempt."

"Then, I shall see you at the theatre."

"Very good."

He chuckled at the uncertainty in her voice. Again, he tipped his hat to the closed carriage door and watched it drive away before continuing on his way home to prepare for an evening of entertainment – and a play.

Acknowledgements

There are many who have had a part in the creation of this story. Some have read and commented on it. Some have proofread for grammatical errors and plot holes. Others have not even read the story and a few, I know, will never read it. However, their encouragement and belief in my ability, as well as their patience when I became cranky or when supper was late or the groceries ran low, was invaluable.

And so, I would like to say *thank you* to Zoe, Rose, Kristine, Ben, and Kyle, as well as my Sweet Tuesday readers on Patreon and my blog, who followed this story as it developed and waited, as patiently as one might do, from one Tuesday to the next to read a new chapter. I feel blessed through your help, support, and understanding.

I have not listed my dear husband in the above group because, to me, he deserves his own special thank you, for, without his somewhat pushy insistence that I start sharing my writing, none of my writing goals and dreams would have been met.

Other Leenie B Books

You can find all of Leenie's books at this link
bit.ly/LeenieBBooks
where you can explore the collections below

~*~

Other Pens, Mansfield Park

~*~

Touches of Austen Collection

~*~

Nature's Fury and Delights, Sweet Regency
Romance Novelette Anthologies

~*~

Dash of Darcy and Companions Collection

~*~

Marrying Elizabeth Series

~*~

Willow Hall Romances

~*~

The Choices Series

~*~

Darcy Family Holidays

~*~

Darcy and... An Austen-Inspired Collection

About the Author

Leenie Brown has always been a girl with an active imagination, which, while growing up, was both an asset, providing many hours of fun as she played out stories, and a liability, when her older sister and aunt would tell her frightening tales. At one time, they had her convinced Dracula lived in the trunk at the end of the bed she slept in when visiting her grandparents!

Although it has been years since she cowered in her bed in her grandparents' basement, she still has an imagination which occasionally runs away with her, and she feeds it now as she did then — by reading!

Her heroes, when growing up, were authors, and the worlds they painted with words were (and still are) her favourite playgrounds! Now, as an adult, she spends much of her time in the Regency world, playing with the characters from her favourite Jane Austen novels and those of her own creation.

When she is not traipsing down a trail in an attempt to keep up with her imagination, Leenie resides in the beautiful province of Nova Scotia with her two sons and her very own Mr. Brown (a wonderful mix of all the best of Darcy, Bingley, and Edmund with a healthy dose of the teasing Mr. Tilney and just a dash of the scolding Mr. Knightley).

Connect with Leenie

E-mail:
LeenieBrownAuthor@gmail.com
Facebook:
www.facebook.com/LeenieBrownAuthor
Blog:
leeniebrown.com
Patreon:
https://www.patreon.com/LeenieBrown
Subscribe to Leenie's Mailing List:
Book News from Leenie Brown
(bit.ly/LeenieBBookNews)